J. T. EDSON'S
FLOATING OUTFIT

The toughest bunch of Rebels that ever lost a war, they fought for the South, and then for Texas, as the legendary Floating Outfit of "Ole Devil" Hardin's O.D. Connected ranch.

MARK COUNTER was the best-dressed man in the West: always dressed fit-to-kill. THE YSABEL KID was Comanche fast and Texas tough. And the most famous of them all was DUSTY FOG, the ex-cavalryman known as the Rio Hondo Gun Wizard.

J. T. Edson has captured all the excitement and adventure of the raw frontier in this magnificent Western series. Turn the page for a complete list of Berkley Floating Outfit titles.

J. T. EDSON'S
FLOATING OUTFIT
WESTERN ADVENTURES
FROM BERKLEY

CHAPTER ONE

Drop Him Plumb in His Tracks

"Hold hard!" Morton Lewis commanded, *sotto voce*, gesturing with his left hand to his two companions so as to cause them and his big dog to come to a halt. "Either you've lived right all your life, Jimmy, or *Ka-Dih's* looking real favorable on us. We've found him and better placed than I'd dare've hoped. Ease forward, quiet as you've done up to now, so's you can take a look."

"He's *magnificent!*" Geraldine Thatcher enthused, in no louder a tone, and before her slightly older brother could speak, she advanced through the bushes they were traversing until she was able to gaze in the direction indicated by their guide. Her well educated New England accent became redolent of compassion as she went on, "It seems such a shame to kill him."

"There's no shame to it, seeing he's been stalked fair and on foot," Mort corrected, his voice having the lazy drawl of a native born Texan; albeit one from a lower strata of society than the girl and her brother. "'Sides which, he's gone some past his prime and's been run off from his herd on account of it. That being, he'll either get his-self stove up bad by a younger'n' more limber bull for trying to get back in among the cows again, or he'll just go on living alone and growing weaker. Either way, all he's got ahead of him, should we just let you draw him and leave him be, is to wind up getting eaten, while he's still just about alive, by bears, wolves, or maybe even coyotes, soon's he gets slowed down so much by old age he can't fend 'em off hisself and doesn't have no *amigos* around to help him."

"Then he's just what I want for the museum," declared

1

First Lieutenant James Thatcher, 2nd United States' Cavalry.

"You'll have to take him from here," Mort warned. "There's no way we can get closer. Which same's judgement on me, likely. Grandpappy Wolf Runner allus allowed no good *ever* come to folks're *loco* enough to go walking when they've got horses they could've used."

The creature being discussed was a splendid, if no longer young, even-toed ungulate of the scientific order of *Artio-dactyla*. Terrestial, herbivorous mammals, its kind had the third and fourth toes of the fore and hind feet evenly developed, with the tips encased in horny sheaths to support its weight and having present small lateral hooves, otherwise known as "dewclaws." Being a "cud-chewer" it was placed in the class of *Ruminantia* and had a compound stomach which temporarily stored often hastily snatched and always only partially chewed food in the first compartment, or "paunch." Such sustenance was later regurgitated in the form of small pellets to the mouth. Then, having been thoroughly "milled," in the process known as "chewing the cud," this was returned to the second compartment where digestion could be commenced.

Actually a *wisent*, or bison, the animal being studied had become more popularly known to the settlers of the United States and Canada as a "buffalo."[1] Despite being exceeded in *height* by the Alaskan elk—just as wrongly designated a "moose"—in other respects it was the largest land dwelling wild animal native to the sub-continent of North America.

Standing some six foot in height at the shoulder and slightly more than double that in length, the bull buffalo[2] in question weighed over two thousand pounds. Due to the great elongation of bony spurs on the backbone at that point,

1. *The only genuine wild buffalo in the world are the "Indian" species,* Bubalus Bubalis, *found in Asia and the Cape and dwarf forest varieties,* Cyncerus Caffer *and* C.C. Nanus, *of Africa. Those running wild in Australia are formerly domesticated animals which have escaped and turned feral.* J.T.E.
2. *To avoid confusion, we will continue to employ the generally accepted American name for the bison.* J.T.E.

the shoulders were high and humped. The massive head and deep, muscular neck were slung low on the shoulders. Yet the rest of the body, notably the hindquarters, were suprisingly narrow in cross-section. Its forequarters, including the head and neck, were covered with a mantle of thick, shaggy hair that terminated abruptly below the knees of the forefeet and just behind the shoulders. While not in fresh "pelage," the coat was still a dark chocolate brown, becoming almost black on the head and shoulders and showed no sign of fading to the pale yellowish-brown coloration it would have acquired by the time the spring molt came around. A long black beard hung from its chin and the tail was short with a tassel of long hair at the tip. Staring, seemingly without expression, the eyes were placed low down on the sides of the head. Above them, indicating it belonged to the family, *Bovidae,* the short, stout horns—each close to twenty-three inches long and having a circumference of seventeen inches at the base—consisted of hollow horny sheaths growing over round bony cores which were never shed and curved outwards and upwards.

The three human watchers in the concealment of the bushes were fairly good representatives of the species, *Homo Sapien.*

Tallish for a member of her sex, curvaceous without allowing this to become blatantly obvious, Geraldine was in her early twenties. She had honey blonde hair, at that moment tucked up inside the low crown of a wide brimmed tan J. B. Stetson hat. Pretty in a frank, open way, her freckled face had already taken on a tan due to an exposure to more sun that she was accustomed to experiencing in Maine. She wore a lightweight brown two-piece riding costume, an open necked blouse of the olive-drab hue given the name "khaki" by British soldiers serving in India, and sturdy black boots suitable for walking over fairly rough terrain. A thin leather pouch, about three feet square and holding materials for drawing, was suspended by a strap from her left shoulder to the right hip. In a close topped military holster on the belt around her waist was a Colt 1853 Navy Model revolver. Using it at extemporized targets, she had proved to be a reasonably good shot.

A couple of years older and somewhat taller, his build good and implying excellent physical condition, Jimmy Thatcher showed a strong family resemblance in his features and the color of his hair. More tanned, as a result of having spent the past two years in Texas with his regiment, he was clean shaven and well groomed, if dishevelled by passing through the bushes. Except for having retained his black Hessian leg service boots and weapon belt, being on furlough, he had changed his uniform for the kind of clothing worn by cowhands. The revolver in his high riding cavalry holster was a walnut handled Colt 1860 Army Model with a seven and a half inch "Civilian" pattern barrel. However, for hunting, he was carrying a single shot Sharps New Model of 1866 rifle which he had had equipped with certain improvements to the original design when it was purchased.

Having just passed his twenty-sixth birthday, Mort Lewis had an advantage over the lieutenant of two inches in height. A wide brimmed hat, its low crown altered to the fashion of Texas and its original white weathered to a yellowish-grey color, hung suspended on his broad shoulders by its fancy leather *barbiquejo* chinstrap. Straight and black, his hair was short and he too had shaved that morning. There was a slightly aquiline cast to his deeply bronzed, ruggedly handsome features and a somewhat Mongoloid slant to his dark eyes indicative of—as he had mentioned when referring to his maternal grandfather—his birthright being part Indian.

Lean of waist, Mort exuded a rawboned fitness and vitality. Encircling his throat, a tightly rolled dark blue bandana trailed its ends over the front of an open necked tartan shirt. As he was acting as guide on a hunting trip, instead of working the range on his small ranch in Holbrock County, the legs of his yellowish-brown Nankeen trousers were tucked into the calf high leggings of *Kweharehnuh* Comanche moccasin. While the garments showed signs of much recent usage, this was not their invariable condition. In fact, like the majority of cow-hands—a canard created by a later generation not-withstanding—he washed, shaved, kept his hair cut and attire as clean as circumstances allowed at all times. A walnut handled Army Colt with a standard eight inch barrel rode the open topped Western style fast draw holster on the right side of his gunbelt and a staghorn hilted J. Russell and Co. "Green River" knife with an eight inches long, clip point blade hung in its Indian-made sheath on the left. Resting across the crook of his left arm, the Spencer repeating carbine he carried, to support his client if necessary, was covered by a long fringed buckskin case inscribed with medicine symbols announcing he was a member of the Antelope band of the Comanche nation. He was equally competent, if not exceptional, in the use of each weapon.

Lying not too far from its master, where it had gone when the party halted, the big dog showed no discernible interest in the proceedings. Coming from a strain created by an Army officer whose education had instilled him with a deep respect for *Ivanhoe*, by Sir Walter Scott, its conformation had derived from careful cross-breeding of Scottish deerhounds and British bull mastiffs to achieve the best each could offer. Shaggy coated and greyish in color, while possessing some of the speed and stamina of the former, it also had some of the bulk and powerful jaws attributable to the latter. Answering to the name, "Pete," it was in its prime and had been of the greatest use to Mort as guard and helper on hunts for stock-killing predators. It had also proved of assistance in the task upon which he was currently engaged.

Asked by an officer who had been a good friend in the days when he had ridden as a civilian scout for the 2nd Cavalry, Mort had agreed to act as guide for the Thatchers on a hunting trip which was to obtain good specimens of Western animals for a museum being established in their home town. His belief that Captain Patrick Kelley would not have made the request unless confident they would get along had soon been justified. Despite it being her first trip west of the Mississippi River, Geraldine had proved to be accustomed to an outdoor life and was willing to accept less than the comforts to which her home in Maine had made her accustomed. Nor had Mort found anything objectionable about his relationship with her brother.

Having formed his liking for the Thatchers, Mort had warned them that acquiring the requisite trophies presented problems, as not all were any longer easy to come by. Already hunting for hides and tongues, along with the need to clear the grazing land for more easily controlled and commercially acceptable cattle, had reduced the formerly massive herd of buffalo in Texas to what a later generation would call, "a point of no return." Much the same applied to the Mexican sub-species of bighorn sheep and pronghorn, often wrongly referred to as an "antelope," Arizona wapiti—misnamed "elk"—the Texas flat-headed grizzly and black bear, all of which had once been numerous in the western regions of the Lone Star State.

Despite the gloomy picture he had painted, Mort had said he could take the Thatchers into an area which still offered a reasonable chance of securing the trophies they required. Being in the wild country over which the *Kweharehnuh* Comanche still retained control, having declined to accept the peace treaty which was concluded at Fort Sorrel,[3] assigning the other bands of their nation to reservations, it was generally regarded as being unsafe for white people to go there.[4] However, as grandson of Chief Wolf Runner, he could enter accompanied by friends. For all that, knowing the nature of the Antelope warriors—rugged individualists like every member of the *Nemenuh,* therefore prone to acting as their respective will desired rather than conforming to laid down rules—he had tried to persuade the girl to remain in the safety of the trading post owned by Sanchez Riley on the fringes of the territory. Saying she had had her expenses paid by the museum to come to Texas and paint pictures of the animals in their natural surroundings, she

3. *Information regarding the negotiation of the peace treaty at Fort Sorrel is given in:* SIDEWINDER. *J.T.E.*
4. *Although it was not generally known at that period, a group of fugitives from justice had been allowed to settle and build a town in another part of the* Kweharehnuh *country, which other wanted outlaws could visit providing certain conditions were met. See:* HELL IN THE PALO DURO *and* GO BACK TO HELL. *J.T.E.*

considered herself obligated to do so and refused to accept his precaution. Having found her to be a most determined young woman, in a polite and friendly way, he had agreed that she should accompany himself and her brother.

Compared with some of the hunting parties which were becoming fashionable with visiting foreign dignitaries and wealthy Easterners,[5] Mort and his companions were traveling light. They rode horses and carried what supplies they would need in a chuckwagon. In addition to his cook from the ranch, who was also an expert skinner, they had only Thatcher's striker with them.

From the beginning, luck had favored the party. Without having needed to go too deep into the *Kweharehnuh* country, the young lieutenant had already taken several very good trophies. What was more, he had quickly earned Mort's approbation by showing a sportsmanship of a high order while taking them. Not for him the easily attained kill, regardless of quality. He had invariably passed up animals which, being an excellent shot, could otherwise have fallen to his rifle without effort because he had not considered them worthy of being exhibited. Furthermore, as soon as he had obtained what he regarded as being a satisfactory specimen, he had declined to take another of its kind, even if one better had crossed their path.

Despite it being the last day before the party must start back to allow him to rejoin his regiment, and having failed to acquire such a specimen, Thatcher had proved less than enthusiastic when told the deductions drawn by Mort from tracks found whilst scouting in a wide circle around their camp that morning. On learning the signs indicated that the quarry would be a bull buffalo of greater than average size, he had said he wondered whether collecting it would offer a sufficiently sporting challenge. Unlike the stalking skill required when taking his Mexican bighorn sheep and Arizona elk, or the courage called for to tackle the grizzly bear he had brought down, according to what he had been told

5. *A description of a party of foreign visitors taking such a trip is given in:* THE BIG HUNT. *J.T.E.*

by older officers, it seemed to him that hunting buffalo was as easy and no more dangerous than shooting fish in a barrel.

Mort had agreed that, although "running" them on horseback was sufficiently hazardous to test courage and skill, there was some justification in the comments when dealing with the animals in a herd. However, they did not apply when a lone bull was the quarry. Separated from its companions and deprived of the sense of security it derived from their company, such a creature could prove as dangerous an antagonist as a grizzly bear. Keeping constantly alert and made nervous by its solitary state, it would not hesitate before charging, whether approached on foot or horseback. When that happened the speed and surprising agility of its massive body combined with its great size, made taking one far from a sinecure.

Most impressed by the grave way in which his experienced young guide had imparted the information, the lieutenant had lost all his qualms over the ethics of embarking upon the hunt. In fact, contemplating its potential danger, he had suggested that his sister stayed behind while Mort and he went after the bull. Pointing out that she had been present during the hunt for the grizzly bear, which had proved anything but free of peril, she had insisted on going with them. Conceding she had not been an impediment to them on that occasion, the two young men had given their agreement. In fact, in a curious way, both had come to regard her as something of a good luck charm.

Having ridden while following the tracks until they disappeared into an area covered with fairly dense bushes and scrubby trees, and having then discovered they had not emerged from the bush when they had completed a circle, Mort had suggested the hunt should be continued on foot as otherwise it would put the horses at great risk. Geraldine had refused to remain with their mounts and, as on other occasions, had proved she was able to duplicate their silent approach through the undergrowth until they had come into view of their quarry.

Showing no sign of being aware of the forthcoming fate described by Mort, the bull buffalo was standing in the center of a largish patch of open ground. Scrambling around on its body, rummaging for external parasites and insects, were a couple of brown-headed cowbirds[6] and a black and white magpie. As if knowing they would help augment its comparatively poor vision, somewhat better hearing and excellent sense of smell, the animal was setting about the preparation of the food it had gathered before settling in this secluded spot where it could halt and perform its essential aid to digestion.

As with other members of the *Ruminantia*, the buffalo had no teeth in the front of the upper jaw. It had, however, broad crowned and sharp-edged molars for grinding and milling its herbivorous diet. Having swallowed the ball of grass it had been working upon, there was a slight pause before it brought up another pellet to chew. Depositing this in the cheek, causing a slight yet discernible swelling, it started to chew with a rotary motion on the side of the mouth where the ball had settled. Then the cud was shifted to the opposite side, where the upper and lower teeth took over the task of milling. In this way, as opposed to the action of more primitive cud-chewers such as the camels— which swing the lower jaw in a long sweep from side to side and chew on both at the same time—the process of masticaton was made faster and more efficient.

"Oh hell!" Thatcher protested, after watching for a few seconds. "This's too *easy*. It'll be like shooting an old milk-cow in a meadow!"

"Had we come on him in these bushes, you wouldn't've tooken him for no old milk-cow," Mort replied, having come to know his male companion well enough to have expected some such remark. "And, was I you, I'd made good and sure I put him down first go now we've found him. Should you miss, he'll take off like the devil chased by holy water and, time we've got the horses, it'll be too late in the day to follow his trail. Which, we'll need to ride after him, he

---

6. *Even before the massive reduction to the number of buffalo, the brown-headed cowbird, Molothrus Ater, had acquired its name by having transferred its attentions to cattle as a means of providing food. J.T.E.*

can outrun any man. Or, happen you only wound him, he'll go into the bushes faster'n a scalded cat. Now me, I'm all for acting sporting-like, but following him in there when he's hurting and could've been down out here's closer to being *loco* than sporting." Pausing to let the other consider what he had said, he went on, "Hell, you've stalked him on foot, fair 'n' square, and it's the luck of the game we've found him like he is, instead of some place's d've made getting him harder. Now you just up and kill him clean."

"Where's the best place to hit him?" the lieutenant inquired, accepting the statement as valid and having found the advice of his guide invaluable when taking the other trophies.

"Depends on how you want him," Mort replied and, knowing the young officer was always keen for information, continued, "Hide hunters allus put a bullet through the lungs of the first one they hit, usually a cow, so's she'll just stand there bleeding from the nose and hold the rest of the bunch's attention while he keeps downing more of 'em. Done that way, and he's good enough, he can maybe drop fifty or so all up close enough to make skinning out the 'flints' easy on what his kind call a 'stand.'"[7]

"That's *out!*" Thatcher declared vehemently, but quietly. "Even if there were more of them around I wanted, I wouldn't lung shoot him to get them. I've heard it takes the poor devil minutes to die hit that way."

"It does," Mort confirmed, finding the response in keeping with the character of the lieutenant. "A head shot'll drop him plumb in his tracks. Trouble being, way he's stood and with that old cannon you're toting, the bullet's like to go clear through and bust out the other side, which'll spoil him for mounting."

"How about if I hit him in the heart?" Thatcher suggested.

"It's a real small target," Mort replied. "Which, I know, you're good enough a shot to hit it. Trouble being, he'll

---

7. *A description of how a professional "skin" hunter operated when shooting buffalo for their hides and tongues is given in:* THE BIG HUNT. *J.T.E.*

most likely run fifty or a hundred yards after he's hit and they'll have one hell of a chore hauling him out of those bushes back of him, 'cause that's where he'll be headed and he won't go down until he's well among 'em. You take him with a spine shot."

"A spine shot it is," the lieutenant assented.

"I'd line up with the barrel resting on that branch," Mort suggested, pointing. "You don't have too all fired wide a mark and, good as I know you are, was I you, I'd take all the help I can get to hold a gun that heavy real steady while I was laying them fancy, new-fangled sights on it."

"I'm a good soldier and *always* follow orders," the lieutenant claimed with a smile, aware that the conversation was helping him relax and be the better able to take a careful aim. "When Captain Kelly arranged for me to take this trip, he said I should follow your advice and that's what I'm going to do. Then, if anything goes wrong, you'll be to blame."

"I never yet saw the time when you blue-bellies *didn't* blame the civilian scout for *everything* from flood to hard weather," the guide answered, grinning. "So how's about seeing if you can down that old jasper, afore night comes on us and it's too dark to even find our way back to the horses?"

CHAPTER TWO

He'll Have to be Killed

During the final stages of the quietly spoken conversation, First Lieutenant James Thatcher had moved the sidehammer of his Sharps New Model of 1866 rifle slowly into the fully cocked position so as to reduce the noise of the action being operated. When Morton Lewis stopped speaking, he began to ease the heavy firearm into the position Mort had suggested. Resting the barrel firmly on the junction of a branch and the trunk of a small flowering dogwood tree, he raised the "leaf" backsight just as cautiously, ready to take aim and fire.

An excellent marksman, the young officer was not deterred by the far from simple way in which he had elected to shoot the old bull buffalo. Acting upon the advice of more experienced members of his regiment and possessing sufficient wealth to cater for his whims, he had had the rifle chambered to accept a cartridge of .50 caliber. This had a three and a quarter inch long metal case holding a one hundred and seventy grain powder charge to propel a seven hundred grain bullet patched with a good grade of banknote paper, the use of which improved accuracy and prevented "leading" of the barrel.[1] Even at a much greater range than the one hundred or so yards separating him from his quarry, such a load possessed sufficient power to smash the spine and make an almost instantaneous kill. What was more, the

1. *Although the .50-170-700 cartridge is listed by some authorities as having been introduced in 1875, there is much evidence to prove the "load" had been devised much earlier. This cartridge was not produced by the Sharps Rifle Company, but many of their so-called "buffalo guns" were rechambered for it to order. J.T.E.*

thirty and a quarter inch length of the six groove "rifled"
barrel supplemented the well designed "leaf" rear and blade
foresight in attaining an accuracy which had few equals in
its day.[2] He knew he had acquired the requisite skill to make
the most of its potential.

For all his faith in his own ability, Thatcher refused to
let it lead him into complacent overconfidence. A fine
sportsman, taught to have high standards in such matters,
he respected his quarry too much to want to achieve anything
other than the result he was seeking to attain. Effective as
it was from a "broadside" position, a spine shot offered only
a slender mark at which to sight.

With the butt cradled against his right shoulder and its
weight supported by the improvised rest he was using, the
lieutenant lifted upwards the sliding section of the "leaf"
rearsight which was graduated in intervals of a hundred
yards from one to eight. However, instead of employing the
moveable aperture, he squinted with his right eye through
the notch at the base. Setting the blade of the foresight in
the V-shaped notch, he began to move the barrel until both
were aligned upon his intended mark. Satisfied he was aiming correctly and steadily, his right forefinger began to tighten
smoothly upon the "set" trigger which was another modi-
fication he had had carried out at the factory of the Sharps
Rifle Company.

At which point, fate took a hand!

Having failed to detect the approach of the human beings
and dog, with its avian companions equally unsuccessful in
locating and giving warning of the danger, only something
completely unexpected could have saved the life of the
buffalo!

Such an event occurred!

Skimming low over the bushes, on its way to join the

2. *One of the longest documented hits made by a Sharps .50 caliber rifle
   occurred during the final stages of the Battle of Adobe Walls on June
   the 27th, 1874. Billy Dixon, scout and guide, shot an Indian—claimed
   to have been a senior war chief by some sources—off his horse at a
   distance which was later measured as being* one thousand, five hundred
   and thirty-eight *yards. J.T.E.*

two brown-headed cowbirds and another of its kind, a magpie found itself approaching the girl, two men and dog. Giving vent to a harsh, rattling call of alarm, it twirled aside and upwards. Taking warning, the other black and white feeder and the somewhat smaller pair of birds took off from their perch with wildly fluttering wings.

Equally appreciative of what could be implied by the commotion, the buffalo made no attempt to ascertain the exact nature of the implied danger. Instead, letting out a deep and guttural roar, it commenced one of the rapid turns for which its apparently cumbersome bodily conformation was so well adapted. As it began the movement, it was struck by something which produced a searing pain and caused it to lunge away from its standing position. Building up to the twenty-three or so miles per hour gait at which members of its species could gallop, it plunged into and through the foliage formerly to its rear as if the thickly grown branches did not even exist, much less offer a possible impediment.

The flight could not have been started at a worse moment!

Caught unawares by the unheralded arrival and subsequent behavior of the magpie, Thatcher could not prevent an involuntary reaction. This took place just as the pressure on the set trigger had reached the point where the sear liberated the hammer. Scant though his movement had been, it proved sufficient to ruin the alignment of the rifle's sights he had made. Small though the deflection of the barrel might be, the revised angle at which the bullet flew caused the point of impact to be different to that he had intended. On its arrival, the conical piece of soft lead inflicted a much less fatal wound than he had sought to produce.

There was another adverse result from the magpie having come on the scene!

On being detonated within the confines of a metal cartridge case, the one hundred and seventy grains of prime du Pont black powder turned into an enormous volume of gas. The pressure this exerted whilst driving the bullet ahead of it along the barrel, taking the line of least resistance, created a recoil kick of some magnitude. Even with the rifle grasped firmly, the effect was less than gentle. However, in addition to changing the alignment of the barrel, Thatcher had relaxed his grip just as involuntarily. Driven back, small though the distance might be, the butt plate was slammed against his shoulder with considerable force.

"God damn that 'mother-something,' black and wh—!" Mort Lewis spat out, as a yelp of pain burst from the lieutenant, then realizing what he was saying he brought his tirade to a halt without completing it. Belonging to a generation and philosophy which was not conditioned to believe the employment of profanity in the presence of members of the opposite sex was "trendy" and indicative of a willingness to descend to the conversational level of the "little people", he continued, "Right sorry for what I said, ma'am."

"So am I, although you missed what *I* said," Geraldine Thatcher replied, pleased her own impulsive verbal reaction had not been overheard as she had similar sentiments on the subject. Having given up trying to persuade the guide to address her by her Christian name, she went on, "I let out two words I heard a groom use when a horse kicked him and mama spanked me for repeating. Are you all right, Jimmy?"

"The butt banged my shoulder," Thatcher answered, having lowered the Sharps and started to massage the point of impact. "But I *hit* him!—Didn't you hear the bullet go in, Mort?"

"Can't rightly up and say, 'yes I did,'" the guide answered, then raised a placatory hand as the young officer swung towards him in a manner redolent of indignant belligerance. "Which I'm not saying you *didn't* make a hit. Time's been I've stood along of a feller's was shooting and hadn't heard when he said he had 'n' the critter took off like that ole bull did. Comes us going to take a look, it showed he'd been in the right of it."

"Then let's go and take that look!" Thatcher ordered rather than suggested, forgetting the throbbing ache in his shoulder.

"Why sure," Mort assented. "Only, was I asked, I'd say a one-shooting rifle don't throw lead any too good after it's been fired *once*—Not 'less it's been loaded up again 'fore it gets to be squeezed off at something."

"Sorry, Mort!" the lieutenant apologized with genuine contrition. He realized that a mixture of pain, and annoyance at having failed to make the instantaneous kill he desired, had caused him to forget he was holding a weapon incapable of being fired again until it was reloaded. "Let me shove in another shell, then we'll go and find out whether I'm right or wrong."

"From all I've seen of luffs, blue belly or Johnny Reb, makes no never mind," the guide drawled, his grin robbing the words of any sting despite employing the derogatory term for a first lieutenant. "I'd bet me good drinking money which it's going to be."

Giving a sniff of mock derision, Thatcher replenished the Sharps with ammunition from the pouch attached to the left side of his belt. Then he started to advance from amongst the bushes. At a hand signal from its master, having risen when the magpie caused the disturbance, the big cross Scottish deerhound-British bull mastiff dog moved forward at Mort's side. Accepting the buckskin pouch which had been passed to her, allowing the Spencer repeating carbine to be employed later without the delay of removing it should this become necessary, the girl followed the men.

"*Look!*" Thatcher said eagerly, after having crossed the open ground, gesturing with the barrel of his rifle at a reddish smear on the branches of the bushes amongst which his quarry had disappeared. "That's *blood*. I just *knew* I'd hit him."

"It's blood, for sure," Mort drawled, holding his Spencer ready for instant use. "There's no gainsaying that."

"*But?*" prompted the lieutenant, having come to know his guide very well despite their relatively short acquaintance.

"Way he lit a shuck out of here, I'd say you didn't bust his back like was intended," Mort replied. "Which being, he's hit some other place. Was this heart blood, it'd be some brighter red. Even could he've took off like he did, had he been hit in the lungs, it'd be more clotted up and pinker.

That yellow in it makes him shot in the belly, at a guess."

"*Gut shot!*" Thatcher ejaculated.

"I've heard it called that," the guide admitted in a non-committal tone. "Which it wasn't done deliberate, but come of something we couldn't neither of us have figured on happening."

"He'll have to be killed!" the young officer stated, being aware that—while eventually fatal—such a wound would cause a death which was lingering and excessively painful.

"Something just told me's you'd say *that,*" Mort declared, but there was neither derision nor objection in his voice. Rather it held a timbre of respect for a man who thought the same way he did upon such an important issue and was willing to accept the not inconsiderable risks involved in carrying out the suggestion. "Only there's one thing we've got to settle afore we take off after him."

"What would that be?" Thatcher inquired, bristling with suspicion and determined to refuse any suggestion of him leaving the task to the guide.

"This here's no chore for a danged she-male to be underfoot while you 'n' me's doing it, was I asked," Geraldine guessed, producing a fair recreation of Mort's accent and manner of speech. Then, reverting to her normal voice, she went on, "And *surprising* as some of us might find this, I agree. So you boys can trot along and have your fun. I'll stay here and make a sketch of the buffalo while the way he looked is still fresh in my mind."

"I'd be right tolerable obliged was you to do just that, ma'am," Mort claimed with a smile. "And we'll leave you in peace just's soon's I've fetched the horses so you can mind 'em while we're gone."

"Are you expecting something might happen to them?" Thatcher asked, glancing in concern at his sister.

"I've not seen anything to give me cause to be," the guide answered. "Thing being, apart from bear, wolves and cougar's like horse-meat, this's *Kweharehnuh* country. Which I've never yet run across a brave-heart, be he full *tehnap* or new' started *tuivitsi,* who'd pass up the chance to 'raid' him three fine saddle mounts should he come across them."

" '*Raid*' being what we civilized folk would call, '*steal*,' " the lieutenant said to Geraldine, but did not explain a *tehnap* and a *tuivisti* were respectively an experienced and a recently accepted warrior of the Comanche nation.

"That's about the size of it." Mort confirmed, " 'Cepting, not like said 'civilized folk,' I've never yet knowed a *Nemenuh* to raid from another, even was they from different bands and'd never crossed trails until then."

"I'll go fetch them," the girl offered, starting to remove her drawing case. "There isn't too much daylight left and you could find you've a long chase ahead of you. If you do, you can shout or fire a shot and I'll bring them to you."

"That's a good idea, Gerrie," Thatcher praised, having no doubts about his sister being able to lead the three well trained animals through the bushes from where they had been left hidden. "It will let us start out straight away and save time, Mort."

"I'll float my stick along of you, Jimmie," the guide assented. "Shall I leave Pete here along of you, ma'am?"

"I can't think of any reason why you should," Geraldine refused. "And he'll probably be far more use to you than he will be lying around here doing nothing."

"I hate a woman who will insist upon making good sense," the lieutenant claimed. "How about you, Mort?"

"Now me, I can't put claim to knowing anywhere near so much about women-folk's you allow to, *amigo*," the guide replied laconically. "But one thing I learned good real early was never to answer 'yes' to a fool question like that when said lady's close by 'n' listening. You fetch up the horses, like you said, ma'am. Should we need 'em, we'll loose off three shots with a Colt and you head our way."

"I thought you'd see it *my* way," Geraldine asserted and held out the buckskin pouch. "Do you want this, Mort?"

"No, ma'am," the guide answered, but was not allowed to continue.

"I wounded him, Mort!" Thatcher said grimly, "So it's up to me to finish him off."

"You won't get a whole slew of argument from me on that," the guide drawled. "Only I don't take kind to the notion of traipsing around in there with my Spencer needing uncovering should it be wanted *pronto*. Top of which, even though I haven't seen anything to make me reckon it should happen, should any *Kweharehnuh* come on you and you show it to them, ma'am, they'll know you're with me and leave you be."

"I'll keep it in mind," the girl promised and, as the men turned away, concluded, "Good luck."

"Do you think it's likely to happen, Mort?" the lieutenant asked worriedly, as he and the scout set off through the bushes with the dog ranging a short distance ahead of them.

"Not *likely,* but it could. This's their country and, should any brave-heart happen to be roaming hereabouts, he's certain sure to follow the trail of three riders when he comes on it. Miss Geraldine'll be safe enough with that old medicine boot of mine, though. No *Kweharehnuh,* even a *tuivitsi* all hot and eager to make a name for his'self's going to mess with somebody who's close to Wolf Runner."

"Gerrie was saying, the way you 'Miss Geraldine' and 'ma'am' her all the time, perhaps you don't like her."

"I like her good, Jimmie," Mort corrected and, having no desire to discuss the matter further, sought for a change of subject. Gesturing towards the dog, he went on, "I wish Colonel McDonald'd put some nose hunting blood into ole Pete there. He's a whole heap better at seeing and running down critters than trailing 'em by smelling."[3]

"You've trailed the buffalo this far without having needed to use him," Thatcher pointed out, taking the hint. "And even a blue belly luff like me can make out which way he's gone without needing a fool dog to do it."

"Now it's *real* pleasurable to know there's *one* thing a luff, be he blue belly or Johnny Reb, can do *right,*" Mort declared, the twinkle in his dark eyes belying his seemingly sarcastic tone. However, he continued to look ahead while

3. *While Colonel Iain McDonald, then commanding the 3rd United States Cavalry, was probably working to create the best result of cross breeding from Scottish deerhound and British bull mastiff at the period of the events recorded therein, there was no reference to this activity in the notes from which we produced:* A MATTER OF HONOR *J.T.E.*

he was speaking. "Only I'm all for having things done the easiest way I can."

"I've never yet come across a civilian scout who *wasn't,*" the lieutenant countered, although he too never took his gaze from the bushes before them. "I remember the time one asked me to pull him back from the fire because his feet were burning."

Despite the comments made by the two men, the dog clearly knew what was expected of it. While possessed of a fair turn of speed resulting from its deerhound blood, despite the trail being sufficiently fresh to render unnecessary the increased powers of scent developed in a breed intended for hunting in such a fashion, it did not attempt to dash off at a speed beyond the capability of its human companions. Instead, head raised so as to better employ its eyes and ears in locating the prey they were following, it walked a few feet in front of them. Nor, although a distant crashing of the foliage indicated where the buffalo was to be found, did the dog increase its speed. It looked back a couple of times, but received no signal or verbal command to set off in hotter pursuit and therefore refrained from doing so.

"I could send Pete on to try and pin him down until you catch up," Mort drawled, after having received the second look from the dog.

"That could be dangerous for him in this kind of country, couldn't it?" Thatcher guessed, having had experience of working with hounds after dangerous quarry. "Out on the range, he'd have room to move around, but not in here. Should he get into trouble, he'd have nobody to help take the bull's attention from him."

"Like you say," Mort agreed. "It'd be a whole heap safer for him in here was he running with a pack, so's there'd be more of 'em on hand to back him up."

"Then I'd rather you kept him close enough for us to do it," the lieutenant stated, looking forward without discerning any indication of approaching the fringe of the bushes. "It's gone quiet ahead!"

"Sure. Could be he's come to open ground."

"Or he could have stopped in the bushes to rest his wound?"

"There's that."

"I've never been one for gambling," Thatcher said, as his companion glanced at the dog. "So leave us keep Pete where he is until we know which one it is."

Nodding in approval, Mort did not give the command which would have sent the dog onwards faster than he and the lieutenant could follow. Despite the absence of noise, and Pete's lack of "nose" notwithstanding, there was no difficulty deciding in which direction to go. Close to two thousand pounds of buffalo dashing heedlessly through had left sufficient signs of its passage to render visual tracking simple. For all that, Mort restrained the eagerness of his young companion. Knowing there could be a need for very steady and accurate shooting should they come upon their quarry unexpectedly in such terrain, which would be difficult enough to achieve without being short of breath, he insisted upon maintaining a much slower pace than Thatcher sought to employ.

"God damn it to hell and back the short way!" the guide grumbled, as the party entered a smaller clearing than that in which they had first seen their quarry, after having covered about half a mile. "Even had Pete a nose like a bluetick coonhound, it wouldn't help him sic 'em in country like this. What wind there is's coming from every which way at once!"

"He went straight on over, though," Thatcher replied, indicating with his Sharps where a bush had been flattened on the opposite side of the open ground. "It must be clear not far ahead."

"Happen it is and he's still moving, we'll call up Miss Geraldine with the horses and turn Pete loose on him," the guide decided. "I'm getting quick-sick of all this fool walking."

Holding the weapons in the position of readiness known to soldiers engaged in bayonet fighting training as the "high port," the two young men continued to follow the slowly moving dog while they were talking. Suddenly, head swinging around, Pete came to a halt. The bark which left the dog was drowned by a loud, shrill whistling sound which resembled the explosive hissing made by high pressure steam suddenly released from a locomotive.

Almost as if it had known who was responsible for its suffering, the buffalo burst from its place of concealment well to the left of its original exit from the clearing and rushed towards the young officer!

CHAPTER THREE

The Barrel's Plugged

Acting under the impulse of well trained reflexes rather than conscious mental guidance, despite the fact that he had been taken as unawares as he had when startled by the magpie, First Lieutenant James Thatcher swung towards the on-coming buffalo with his Sharps New Model of 1866 rifle rising towards the firing position. While doing so, he noticed that the big shaggy grey dog had dropped into a crouching posture instead of going to meet the other animal. Knowing this was not caused by fear, but to avoid entering the line of fire, he realized it was making his own task easier. How-ever, at that moment, he had other matters of greater im-portance and urgency demanding his attention than thinking about the high standard of obedience Pete was displaying.

Due to the state of exhilaration he had been experiencing and the interest aroused whilst seeking out the buffalo, the young officer had lost all awareness of the throbbing ache in his shoulder caused by the improperly controlled recoil kick when he had fired and wounded the animal. A com-bination of having held his right arm in practically the same position all the time he was on the move and the sudden motions he was now making brought the pain flooding back. The sensation was so severe, it overrode the surge of ex-citement caused by the sight of his quarry and the appre-ciation of the danger in which its unexpected behavior was placing him.[1]

1. *The habit of circling back and, waiting in concealment for its pursuers, when injured and being followed, is common amongst all wild species of the* Bovidae. *Such incidents have frequently been recorded as hap-*

A gasp burst from Thatcher and he could not restrain an equally involuntary flinching away as the metal butt plate touched him. This caused his right forefinger to tighten before he was ready and put the set trigger into operation. Once again, the discharging of a bullet sent the recoil driving against his incorrectly positioned shoulder. This time, however, the force seemed even more intensified by the already suffering flesh upon which the impact arrived. He found himself unable to hold back the cry of pain which it elicited. Nor could he prevent himself from going in a staggering spin to collide with Morton Lewis, who was moving around ready to supply any support he might need. Fortunately, his instincts as a hunter caused him to tighten the second and third fingers of his left hand upon the cartridge they were carrying to prevent a re-occurrence of his having neglected to reload at the larger clearing. From what was happening, this precaution seemed likely to be justified.

"Pete!" the guide yelled, as he was sent reeling by the impact and the Spencer repeating carbine was knocked from his grasp to fall muzzle first on the ground.

Instantly, upon hearing the voice of its master, knowing what was required, the dog rose from its crouch and, giving a roaring bark, darted forward!

Seeing Pete approaching, the buffalo responded as it would when confronted by a wolf. Instead of continuing to charge, it skidded to a halt and lowered its head as far as the stubby neck would allow to give its horns full play. This was what Pete wanted, but he did not rely solely upon it to delay the attack upon the human beings. Instincts from far distant British bulldog ancestors—vastly different from the oddly shaped and wheezing creatures bearing the name in modern show rings—which had not been eradicated by the

pening with Cape and Indian buffalo, the guar of Asia, and even the feral buffalo of Australia. However, as hunting on foot and following up wounded animals, as Morton Lewis and First Lieutenant James Thatcher were doing, only rarely happened in the United States of America, the bison was not so well known for laying ambushes in this fashion. J.T.E.

original matings with English mastiffs to supply greater size and the more recent admixture of Scottish deerhound blood, supplied the best answer to such tactics.

Deftly slowing his approach, the big dog suddenly lunged, and its powerful jaws grabbed its quarry by the nose. Like most of the *Bovidae* (the reason why a ring through the nostrils is such an effective way of controlling a recalcitrant domestic bull) this was a most tender spot for the buffalo. Therefore, having obtained the grip—which went back to the time when one section of its ancestors were employed to assist butchers in slaughtering cattle—the attack was serving a similar purpose.

By taking a good stance, with its legs spread wide apart, the dog prevented the buffalo from getting sufficient purchase with the head to toss it off. Snorting in fury, the bull plunged forward, trying to dash Pete against one of the small bushes with which the clearing was speckled. Alert to the possibility, the dog swung its hindquarters clear at the last moment and did not relax its hold.

"God damn it!" Mort ejaculated furiously, having snatched up his Spencer and, without needing to think what he was doing, taken the precaution of checking before attempting to use it. "The barrel's plugged. You'll have to take him, Jimmie!"

Hearing the words, Thatcher forced himself to act regardless of the pain from his shoulder. Thrusting down the triggerguard caused the breechblock of the Sharps to descend and eject the spent cartridge case. Then, gritting his teeth as his right hand was compelled to accept the full weight, he replaced it with the round he was holding in the left. With this done, and the left hand returned to the foregrip, the right raised the triggerguard to its normal position. Pulling back the hammer, face set in lines of grim determination, he once more brought up the rifle. Instantly, the pressure of the butt plate against his shoulder intensified his suffering. For all that, he forced himself to concentrate upon holding the Sharps steady and taking aim. As he was doing so, a resurgence of excitement engendered by the dangerous situation drove off the pangs which were assailing him.

"Get Pete away!" the lieutenant gasped.

"Yo!" Mort assented in the fashion of the cavalry, trying to clear the muzzle of the Spencer with his left forefinger. "Pete. Leave it!"

Obedient to the command, the big dog opened its jaws. Relief caused the buffalo to throw up its head as its nose was set free from the painful grip. Making the most of the respite granted, Pete bounded clear and came to a halt ready to return to the attack if needed.

Watching along the barrel, with sights aligned on their intended mark, Thatcher waited until the head of the buffalo began to lower. Then he squeezed the trigger and the Sharps bellowed. Instantly, the thrust of the recoil brought back the pain which he had put from his mind. Gasping in agony, eyes filling involuntarily with tears and obscuring his vision, he retreated a couple of hurried steps and could not retain his grip on the rifle with either hand.

The loss of the Sharps did not prove as dangerous as would have been the case if it had happened on the previous occasion the lieutenant had fired!

Struck in the center of the forehead, its brain shattered by the onwards passage through the skull, the buffalo crumpled and went down as if suddenly boned. Its legs kicked spasmodically a few times, but this was merely the involuntary reactions of muscles in an already lifeless body. Despite the disadvantage under which he had fired, Thatcher had at last achieved the result of which he had been earlier robbed.

"Nice shot, *amigo!*" Mort praised. "How bad is it?"

"Hurts like hell," the lieutenant replied, brushing his eyes clear with the back of his left hand while tentatively working the right shoulder and arm. "But I don't think anything's broken."

"There's some's might say it's justice on you for shooting off a cannon that ways 'stead of using a wheel-carriage like sensible folks," the guide drawled, walking forward. "Let me see how bad it looks."

"Thanks for the sympathy," Thatcher sniffed, having detected the note of relief underlying the reference to his Sharps. Laying it down, he opened and carefully pulled away the front of his shirt, continuing, "I hope it doesn't look as bad as it feels, not that *that* is possible."

"It's bruised to hell and gone," Mort diagnosed, studying the purplish-black discoloration of the skin which was spreading across the lieutenant's right shoulder. "And it's going to get some worse afore it starts coming better."

"I thought it *might!*" Thatcher gritted, directing a baleful glare at the rifle. "Damned if I don't give the mule-kicking son-of-a-bitch to some *deserving* friend like *you* and, should I do it, you'll find I'm no Indian-giver where it's concerned."

"You sound like you're tolerable annoyed with that fine, straight shooting old rifle," the guide remarked, but made no attempt to refute the popular conception that Indians tended to request the return of any present they might make. Instead, although there was little discernible change in his voice and demeanor, he became serious as he continued, "Which I reckon the best thing we can do is take you on over to Grandpappy Wolf Runner's village. Ole Healing Hands, him being a better'n fair medicine man, will quick enough take the worst of the pain out of your hurtings."

"Is the village near by?"

"Should you be able to keep up, I reckon we could make it there by midnight at the latest."

"How about Gerrie and the buffalo?"

"Was figuring we could take her back to the wagon and tell Clay where to come 'n' skin him out," Mort replied. "Way you hit him 'tween the eyes, I don't reckon the bullet'll've spoiled his head over much. With that done, they can head for Sanchez Riley's and you 'n' me'll either catch up with them there, or along the trail to the stage relay station."

"That sounds good to *me*," the lieutenant declared, remembering how his sister had mentioned hopes of visiting an Indian village which was not on a reservation so that she could sketch its occupants. "But I wonder whether Gerrie will go along with doing it?"

CHAPTER FOUR

You're a Mystery to Me

Deciding she had completed the pencil sketch of the buffalo bull to her satisfaction and would be able to duplicate it in oil paints on returning home, Geraldine Thatcher removed it from the stiffened back of the leather carrying case. Having put it into the compartment where it would be kept flat and clean, she inserted a fresh sheet of white paper. Making herself comfortable upon the saddle she was using as a seat, she set about creating what she hoped would prove an equally lifelike reproduction of Morton Lewis.

As her brother and their guide had anticipated, the girl had experienced little difficulty in collecting the horses. Fastening them one behind another, she had led them through the bushes to the clearing. Having no idea how long the men would be away, but suspecting they would not return too soon, she had decided she and the animals might as well be as comfortable as possible. After fitting the set of hobbles each carried in its saddlebags, she had removed the rigs and bridles to allow them to rest and graze unencumbered. Leaving them to fend for themselves, knowing they could not wander far and were unlikely to quit the open ground, she had turned her attention to the sketching which was one of her main interests in life. However, before commencing, she had taken the Colt Navy Model of 1853 revolver from its holster and placed it within reaching distance. It was not that she had lacked faith in the assurance given by Mort, but she felt the precaution was advisable in case any predatory animals should be attracted to the possibility of a meal of horse-flesh.

While working, Geraldine had listened for any indication that the mounts were required by her brother and the guide. She had heard nothing to suggest this might be the case while she was working to reproduce the appearance of the bull buffalo. Nor had any suggestion that the horses could be required reached her ears as her pencil moved over the paper and an excellent "head and shoulders" likeness of Mort began to take form.

Looking up from the sheet of paper upon which she was working, the girl sighed. Being very skillful at her hobby, she had contrived to catch more than just the basic lines of her subject's face. There was an indication of his rugged independence and competence. Yet she had also produced something which underlaid his self-confident exterior. Just what this might be, she had never been able to decide. Yet she knew that, in some way, it involved her.

"I don't know, Mort," Geraldine mused. "You're a mystery to me!"

Although her generation had not been encouraged to believe casual sexual intercourse at every opportunity was the ultimate in human achievement, the girl had found the guide a most interesting man. Her feelings had not arisen from a desire to discover how he might perform as a bed-mate, but because he was a person far outside her previous experience. In many ways, he was far more knowledgeable than she would ever be. Yet, in others, she sensed he was as unknowing and vulnerable as a child. Since they had met, he had behaved with politeness and courtesy; but he had always kept her at a distance, steadfastly refusing even to come to first name terms with her as he quickly had with her brother.

At first, Geraldine had wondered whether the guide objected to having a woman forced upon him, or believed she would prove a nuisance on the hunting expedition. If so, he had never mentioned it. In fact, he had soon expressed satisfaction over her behavior and willingness to accept the lack of comforts to which she was accustomed. Remembering that her brother had mentioned Mort had had an Indian mother, she wondered if this could be the reason for his attitude towards her. Yet, should this have been the case, he had never made any attempt to conceal his parentage.

Unknowingly, the girl had discovered the reason for the guide declining to become too closely associated with her!

While his father had been a rancher and mustanger, Texas born and raised, and his mother the daughter of a *Kwehar-ehnuh* "name warrior", it was only recently Mort had become subjected to prejudice on account of his mixed blood to any great extent. During his formative years, he had spent his time equally in the company of people of both parents. In addition to having been accepted for his good qualities, he had made many friends amongst each. Then, serving under the command of Colonel John Salmon "Rip" Ford in the Army of the Confederate States,[1] his abilities as a fighting man and the skills learned from the maternal side of his family had earned him the whole-hearted respect of his comrades-in-arms, which had overridden petty considerations of race and religious creed.

A similar state of affairs had existed when, needing to earn money in the impoverished conditions prevailing after the War Between The States, he had acted as a civilian scout for the 2nd United States' Cavalry. Their duties had been concerned solely with the policing of the border country along the Rio Grande, fending off the depredations of *bandidos* and Indians from Mexico who had grown accustomed to finding easy pickings in Texas during the years of the War. As he had not been helping in any way to enforce the worst aspects of "Reconstruction", imposed by corrupt "carpet-bagger" politicians given control of the State and its disfranchised white populations by the Federal Govern-

---

1. *Ironically, due to the slowness of communications having delayed news of peace reaching him, Colonel John Salmon "Rip" Ford and his troops won the final battle of the War Between the States for the South. However, this took place at Palmitto Hill, some fifteen miles east of Brownsville, Cameron County, Texas, on May the 13, 1865. More than a month earlier, on April the 9th, at the Appamattox Courthouse, the surrender of General Robert E. Lee on behalf of the Confederate States should have signified an ending of all military hostilities. J. T. E.*

ment,[2] he had avoided the stigma which might otherwise
have accrued amongst his fellow Texans over his having
taken such a form of employment.

Nor had Mort been made to suffer on account of his
mixed parentage when the death of his father had brought
him back to run their small VL ranch. Neighbors of long
standing, with one exception, the local ranchers and cowhands were more concerned with making use of his specialized talents when helping them deliver herds of cattle
to what few markets were available, and in hunting down
four-legged predators preying upon their livestock to care
that his mother had not been white. Even the antipathy of
the exception did not have its basis on prejudice as such.
A bitter, crabbed and unpleasant man, old Dexter Chass
disliked every other human being—with the possible ex-
clusion of his only offspring—on principle. Although re-
senting all who lived anywhere near him with an equal
impartiality, he had never forgiven Victor Lewis for having
arrived first and settled upon land with water rights he craved,
regardless of the fact that he had always been allowed access
to the latter. He had turned the hostility he felt from the
dead father to the living son.

Furthermore in those days, the few occupants of what
was then no more than a small hamlet without an official
name—being referred to locally as, "Holbrock's", after its
most affluent citizen—in the center of that section of the
range had never raised the slightest objections to the presence of Mort on their respective premises. To them, he had
been another source of revenue in an area which provided
an all too diminutive amount of available trade. One, moreover—despite a penchant of joining in the wild fun and
games of the cowhands—who could pay for his purchases
with negotiable cash.

Not until a more profitable means of exploiting the enormous number of half longhorn cattle—which had been al-

---

2. *How the life of one man was ruined by the worst aspects of the "Reconstruction" period in Texas is described in:* THE HOODED RID-
ERS. *J.T.E.*

lowed to breed and multiply practically unmolested by human beings during the four years of civil conflict—was discovered and commenced,[3] had the situation begun to change for the worse as far as Mort was concerned. In fact, at the very time when he should have started to enjoy the benefits which had accrued as a result of all his hard work and the risks he had taken, he had discovered this was not to be.

Regrettably, the improvement in the financial conditions of the Lone Star State in general had come too late for many of the local population to benefit. Tired of struggling to make ends meet, when compelled for want of more lucrative markets to sell their cattle to hide and tallow factories for around four dollars a head with calves thrown in free,[4] several of the ranchers had decided to call it quits when offered cash "on the barrelhead" for their respective spreads.

All of the properties had fallen into the control of one man!

How David Masefield Stewart had come by the not inconsiderable amount of money with which he made the purchases was never asked. Or, if it had been, those who sought information upon so personal a matter had not divulged the answer to others. His methods of making the acquisitions had not been open to criticism. Although he frankly admitted his origins were north of the Mason-Dixon line and that he had served the North during the War, he had no apparent connections with the administration of Governor "Carpet-bag" Davis and the "Reconstructionists". Furthermore, all things considered, he had paid a fair price for each ranch.

However, the men whom Stewart had used to replace

3. *How this exploitation of what was then the major natural resource available in Texas was developed—it would be many years before "black gold", oil, became of considerable importance in the economy of the Lone Star State—is recorded in:* GOODNIGHT'S DREAM, FROM HIDE AND HORN *and* SET TEXAS BACK ON HER FEET. *J.T.E.*

4. *For a description of the way in which such a factory was operated, see:* THE HIDE AND TALLOW MEN. *J.T.E.*

such cowhands who had objected to working for a Yankee—
and they were in the majority, at each spread he obtained—
were not of their easy-going and tolerant kind. Obviously
selected as much for their ability to handle dissension against
his wishes as for merely working on the range, the replace-
ments qualified for the name that John Chisum—already a
"cattle baron" of less than savory repute[5]—referred to with
false joviality as "warriors". Therefore, Stewart's predilec-
tion for hiring men of that kind had been regarded with
something close to suspicion by Mort, whose property—
along with that owned by Chass—was all he had not acquired in the area. Not that the Yankee had given any hint
of wanting to add their spreads to his holdings, but the two
properties were essential should he wish to increase the land
already under his control. Regardless of the original misgivings he had caused, and while his pleasant attitude had
not been duplicated by all his men, he had always treated
Mort in a friendly fashion and never hesitated before asking
advice in matters pertaining to the cattle business.

It was, in part, at the instigation of Stewart that Mort
was accompanying the Thatchers on the hunting trip!

The changes amongst the local population had not been
restricted to the ranches. Attracted by the prospect of being
able to make a good profit as conditions in the Lone Star
State improved, other newcomers had arrived. Town dwellers by preference and vocation, they too had their origins
in the northern and eastern States and set themselves up in
a variety of trades of professions. Finding the hamlet had
offered an ideally central location, they had established their
homes and businesses there. This had caused it to grow into
a thriving, if not yet overlarge, town with—although the
man in question was now dead—the name changed to "Holbrock". It had, furthermore, been elevated to the status of
"seat" for a newly created county of the same name and

---

5. *In addition to being featured prominently in the first two books to which
we refer in* Footnote 3 *of this* Chapter, *further information regarding
the less than savory activities of John Chisum can be found in:* THE
MAN FROM TEXAS *and* Part One, "They Called Him The Cattle
King", SLAUGHTER'S WAY. *J.T.E.*

now could boast a sheriff, who also served as town marshal, to enforce its law and order.

However, while the newcomers catered for a variety of needs and luxuries which the hamlet had been too limited in scope to offer, removing the necessity of traveling to some more populous region when such commodities were required, they too were not like the native Texans they had supplanted. Most of them were lacking in the open hearted acceptance of a man for what he was, rather than on account of his wealth or lineage, characteristic of people sharing common bonds of survival against the many perils of the vast frontier lands west of the Mississippi River in general, and amongst cowhands of Texas in particular. Frequently professing their stout Christian beliefs, these were of the kind where charity began at home and, in all too many cases, that was where it also ended.

Despite having shown themselves willing and even eager to accept the trade put their way by Mort while establishing their businesses, later—particularly when references to his already long dead mother began to circulate—the new citizens of the town, especially the wives, had refused to consider him as a social equal. Never a seeker after their company, or even desirous of attaining their acceptance socially, at first he had not been worried by their attitude. He had, in fact, derived a certain sardonic amusement from noticing how those with whom he dealt were still far from slow in taking advantage of the trade he was putting their way.

Being of a more tolerant nature than those responsible for the prejudices, Mort had conceded there might be just cause for some of the misgivings directed his way. Cowhand horseplay, in which he had frequently indulged along with friends from other ranches, was rarely appreciated by the staid town dwellers in any area. Nor had the citizens of Holbrock been any more enamored of the more serious brawls which occurred when he had come into contact with some of the new men hired by Stewart. In each case, it had been established by Sheriff Jerome Dickson—as honest and fair a peace officer as ever pinned on a badge, despite having been appointed by the Governor—and accepted by their employer, that he was not the instigator of the fracas. However, being new to the West and its ways, the citizens might have assumed there was no smoke without fire. Certainly, possessing a streak of stubborn pride in his make-up, he had never backed away when threatened or abused. Instead, he had demonstrated—if less lethally than might have been the case, considering his Comanche upbringing—a fighting ability as rough as anything employed against him.

If it had not been for meeting with Rose Humboldt, Mort would have paid no attention to the way in which the newcomers regarded him. However, they had been attracted to one another from the beginning and their feelings had blossomed into love. Being a man of honor, trained to respect such proprieties, he had made no attempt to conceal this state of affairs from her parents. Despite having what many people would have considered reasonable prospects, on having broached the subject with her father, he was ordered never to set foot upon the Humboldt property again—in terms which could have brought grave repercussions against the speaker if Mort had not just managed to keep his temper under control—and the girl was sent to stay with an aunt somewhere in New England. Nor had the wrath of the irate father been appeased by these measures. Furious at a "half breed" having had the audacity to seek the hand of his only child in matrimony—and not a little frightened by the danger in which, he sensed, his blistering tirade could have placed him—Brenton Humboldt had began to exert all the power offered by being the most wealthy citizen, justice of the peace and owner of the Mercantile & Cattlemen's Bank of Holbrock, towards persuading the town to turn Mort into a social leper.

Paying a visit to the VL ranch house to discuss business with its owner, David Masefield Stewart had found him in a mood of black depression. On being told of the request to act as guide for the Thatchers, he had advised Mort to accept. He had claimed the absence of four or five weeks, which was all the time the hunting trip would take, would allow the affair to die down, and he had promised to do all he could to smooth things over whilst the other was away. Concluding he was hearing good sense and finding the thought of remaining in the area less than pleasant to contemplate, Mort had sent off his confirmation to accompany First Lieutenant James Thatcher. It had not been until they met that he discovered Geraldine was going with them.

Therefore, in one respect, the girl was correct in assuming Mort had misgivings about her company.

However, the feelings of the guide had little to do with doubting whether she could stand up to the rigors of the trip. That aspect had been settled to his complete satisfaction within twenty-four hours of their meeting. While he had soon found her presence far from unpleasant, unlike members of a later and more pampered generation, his ego did not require the boost of trying to attain a conquest sexually where she was concerned. Furthermore, being surprisingly sensitive under his rugged exterior, he had even shied from letting himself appear too friendly in case his motives should become suspect and be met with an attitude similar to that of Brenton Humboldt on the part of her brother.

Hearing one of the horses give a snort of alarm, Geraldine's thoughts were diverted from Mort!

Looking around without rising, but picking up the Navy Colt almost instinctively, the girl discovered six men were entering the clearing!

Coming from the direction by which Geraldine's party had arrived, the newcomers were on foot.

One was a tall, lean, untidily dressed, albeit well armed white man of unprepossessing appearance!

The others, all carrying weapons, were Indians!

CHAPTER FIVE

They Ain't *Kweharehnuh*

As was only to be expected Geraldine Thatcher experienced a sensation of alarm over the arrival of the six men!

Yet, due to the faith she had in Morton Lewis, the girl found the sight of the five Indians more reassuring than she might otherwise have done considering their unwholesome looking companion!

Studying the latter, Geraldine concluded she would have felt much more perturbed if they had all been white and looked as unsavory as him!

To the untutored gaze of the girl, he appeared to be dressed after the fashion of a cowhand. However, the few she had met during her short time in Texas had invariably treated her with courtesy and respect. Her instincts suggested such an attitude might not be displayed in this case.

Eyes schooled to read the signs of the West would have decided the man was "trouble on the hoof!!"

There were lines of dissipation and implied evil on an aquiline face which, apart from being sallow—almost wax-like—was indicative that he had a proportion of Indian blood. Like Mort, he wore Indian leggings and moccasins, but his headdress was a battered and dirty black Burnside campaign hat. However, his shoulder long, greasy black hair, unshaven and unwashed features, and far from clean clothing had acquired their condition as a result of deliberate neglect to make any improvements. He had a walnut handled Colt 1860 Army revolver tucked butt forward into the right side of a grubby dark blue silk sash about his middle, and a bowie knife hung in an Indian made sheath at the left side of the leather belt which passed around it.

Despite the slight relief she was feeling over their presence, as their attire was so similar to that of the "tame"
braves she had seen on the reservation close to the head-
quarters of the 2nd United States' Cavalry at Fort Bracken,
Geraldine was disappointed by the appearance of the Indians. She had hoped for something much more impressive
from members of the free-ranging *Kweharehnuh* Comanche
who, according to Mort, had so far escaped the "blessings"
of life on a reservation and followed the existence of their
ancestors, albeit in a somewhat restricted fashion.

All the Indians conveyed the impression of being in their
late teens, about half the age of their white companion.
Stockily built, of medium height, they had broad and close
to Mongoloid coppery brown features decorated by patterns
of paint. Their shoulder long black hair was held back by
cloth bands of different colors, and none sported so much
as a single feather as part of his headdress. Despite wearing
castoff white men's jackets or shirts, they had only breech-
clouts of various materials below waist level, leggings and
moccasins. Three carried firearms, but only old single shot
and muzzle loading carbines which necessitated having
powder flasks and bullet pouches suspended about their
persons. The other two were armed respectively with a war
lance and bow and arrows. All had either a knife or a
tomahawk as a side arm.

A significant point, although it escaped the notice of the
girl, was that none of the leatherwork displayed by the
quintet was made from the hide of a pronghorn!

"Good afternoon," Geraldine said, trying to keep her
voice from showing trepidation and holding the Colt Navy
Model of 1853 revolver so it would be in view without
actually being pointed at the new arrivals. "Who are you?"

"Was fixing on asking you the self-same, gal," the white
man answered, his voice a far from pleasant, high pitched
North Texas drawl which contrived to sound subservient yet
somehow menacing.

"I'm a friend of Mort Lewis," the girl announced, watching the men come closer to her at a slow walk, their eyes

darting warily about the clearing. Wishing she could remember the name by which the guide was known to the *Kweharehnuh* Comanche, she went on, "Do you know him?"

"I've heard tell of him," the white man admitted, right thumb hooking into the sash close to the butt of the Army Colt. "He's a half breed, what I've heard. Where's he at right now?"

"He and my brother went after a buffalo bull which was wounded," Geraldine replied. "They sh—*will* be back any moment now!"

"Will, huh?" the man grunted and, despite giving no indication of having noticed the slip almost made by the girl, he slowed his pace to allow the Indians to move ahead of him.

"*Yes!*" Geraldine said, hoping she sounded more confident than she was feeling. Then, recollecting what she had been told by Mort, she gestured with her Colt towards the fringed buckskin pouch which she had draped in plain sight across the seat of his low horn, double girthed Texas range saddle. "He left that with me!"

"Real fancy sort of do-hickey," the man drawled. "Ain't it?"

"You know what it is, of course?" the girl inquired, noticing with growing consternation that none of the Indians had done more than give the pouch a cursory glance and were showing a far greater interest in their surroundings, particularly the three horses.

"Sure I know what it is," the man admitted, in what was clearly intended to be a disinterested fashion even though he was not entirely successful in producing it.

"Mort told me I should show it to any of his mother's people who came along," Geraldine explained, running her gaze from one to another of the newcomers and feeling increasingly alarmed. "Then they would know I'm a friend."

"And that fancy do-hickey'd be the son-of-a-bitch to do her, for sure," the man conceded with a mocking leer. "Trouble being, these bucks of mine are Wacos. They ain't *Kweharehnuh*, nor bound to take notice of Antelope medicine."

Having made the disturbing pronouncement, the speaker

barked a few words in a language which Geraldine could not understand!

Clearly the Indians were able to do so!

Letting out a derisive guffaw, the brave equipped for archery dropped his bow and darted towards the girl. Moving somewhat slower, yet with an equally obvious suggestion of deadly purpose and evil intent, the others retained their respective main armament as they too started to converge upon her. However, the sallow faced white man came to a halt and started to direct glances at the bushes surrounding the clearing. Although he did not draw it, his right hand moved to close about the butt of his revolver.

Concluding the quartet meant mischief and probably much worse, Geraldine discarded the flat leather drawing case. Even as she was starting to rise, she became sickingly aware that it was highly unlikely merely pointing her Colt would frighten her intended assailants. Nor, she realized—even if she could bring herself to shoot at another human being— would she be able to use the weapon quickly enough to deal with all of them.

"It seems you're were right to leave your medicine pouch with Gerrie," First Lieutenant James Thatcher remarked as through the bush, he saw the six men entering the clearing as he and Mort Lewis were making their way there after having dealt with the wounded bull buffalo. "She's got callers!"

"Sure," the guide agreed. "Only, even was they *Kweharehnuh*, which they're *not*, I wouldn't trust them with Waxie Corovan along!"

"*Waxie Coro—!*" the young officer commenced, knowing the man in question to be an unproven gun runner and whiskey peddler.

"Hold hard!" Mort hissed, reaching with his right hand to hold down the the Sharps New Model of 1866 rifle which his companion was starting to raise shoulderwards. "*That* won't serve your sister but to get her killed!"

Having recognized the man wearing mostly white attire, the guide knew Geraldine was in grave danger. Like himself,

Dennis "Waxie" Corovan was part Comanche. There, however, all resemblance ended. Even the other bands of the
Nemenuh did not hold the *Wawai* in high esteem and his
mother had been a "Wormy," as the name could be translated
into English. What was more, the company he was keeping
ruled out any chance of his presence in the clearing having
harmless intent.

Despite being further away, Mort was more successful
than Geraldine Thatcher in identifying the tribe to which
the Indians belonged. Or rather, he knew they were not
Kweharehnuh nor even *Wawai* Comanche. Therefore, taking
into account that all were young and wearing badly applied
war paint, he guessed they had quit some reservation to
search for loot and coups in the manner of their ancestors.
He also realized that, particularly with the chance of acquiring three good quality saddlehorses and the bonus of
molesting a white woman, they would not respect the medicine pouch he had left to indicate her association with him
if any of his mother's people should happen upon her in his
absence.

There was, the guide concluded from his scrutiny of the
Indians, one consolation. Neither they nor Corovan were
carrying anything to indicate they had found the chuck wagon
and had killed the two men with it.

"God damn it!" Thatcher hissed, retaining sufficient presence of mind to hold his voice to the low level he had been
using, but halting the movement of the rifle. "We can't just
stand here—!"

"We're not going to," Mort answered. "Put that ole Sharps
down and get out your belt gun, you'll be able to use it
better."

Being vastly more experienced than his companion, who
had yet to go into action, the guide had instantly seen the
danger of opening fire from their present position. The situation called for caution and not impetuosity. Even if the
party fled as soon as a shot came their way, they would be
unlikely to leave without killing Geraldine. What was more,
in addition to suffering from the disadvantage of needing

to be reloaded by hand for each shot, the Sharps would be more of a liability than an asset to its owner with his right shoulder so badly bruised. Fortunately, as he had proved on targets, he had acquired sufficient competence in using the Army Colt with his left hand provided he was shooting at a much closer range.

"I see you're not leaving your Spencer," the lieutenant remarked, as he turned from leaning his rifle against a bush.

"Could be we'll need a mite more range than the colts give afore we get there," Mort replied. "Let's go—and move quieter than you've ever done it afore."

Regardless of his comment, the guide was aware that his Spencer was only marginally better than the Sharps in the prevailing circumstances. Although the triggerguard-loading lever ejected the spent cartridge case and replenished the chamber from the seven-capacity magazine tube in the butt, the need to cock the hammer manually between shots severely restricted the speed at which it could be fired. For all that, he considered its greater range discounted this factor.

After Thatcher had drawn the revolver with his left hand, the two young men started to advance once more. Given the appropriate order by its master, the big dog followed just behind him in a manner more suited to a wild creature than a domesticated animal.

Moving through the bushes side by side as swiftly as possible while also keeping concealed and avoiding any noise which might betray them, Mort was pleased his companion had attained the requisite skill at stalking to make this possible. However, he was also aware of another factor which was helping to keep them undetected. As he drew closer, he was able to see which tribe the Indians belonged to. Due to the Wacos having been compelled to take up life on a reservation long before such a fate befell the Comanche, the young men had not acquired the skills of more seasoned warriors. For all that, he had no intention of allowing himself to become complacent. To do so could bring about the very thing he was wanting to avert. Even with things going

favorably, he knew saving the girl was still far from a sinecure.

"Only a few more feet!" the guide breathed, in answer
to a glance directed his way by the lieutenant.

Even as Mort uttered the instruction, the matter was taken
from his hands!

Having listened to the conversation between Geraldine
and Corovan, the guide had been grateful for the distraction
it was offering. It had prevented the vastly more competent
lanky man from exercising all his skill and detecting the
danger which was approaching. However, hearing and
understanding what was said to the Indians, Mort realized
he dare not wait to get nearer before taking action.

"Pete!" the guide hissed, starting to bring the Spencer
upwards. "Attack!"

Even as the girl was arriving at her far from palatable
assumptions and beginning to raise the revolver with the
intention of selling her life as dearly as possible, she heard
a snarling bark close to a roar from her rear!

Before Geraldine or any of the men in the clearing could
fully comprehend what was happening, something big and
greyish dashed by her to hurtle upwards!

An instant later, the leading brave was thrown sprawling
on to his back with the powerful jaws of Mort's dog sinking
teeth into his throat!

Confident that Pete would know which of the braves to
tackle, the guide made his own decision. Much as he would
have liked, he did not attempt to fire at Corovan. For one
thing, the lanky man was partially concealed behind the
braves. Therefore, at that moment, he was posing the least
threat to the well being of the girl.

Cradling the butt of the Spencer at his right shoulder, having cocked its hammer while speaking with Thatcher, Mort
sighted and fired. Struck in the center of the chest, having
been selected for the way in which he was armed, the warrior
with the war lance spun around and the lance flew from his
grasp. As was the case with the Comanche, such a weapon
was only carried by a Waco brave determined to prove himself

more courageous than his companions. Therefore, of all the party, he was the most likely to press home his attack regardless of what was being done by his companions. Having used it so effectively, the scout did not take the time required to prepare the carbine for firing again. Tossing it aside, he snatched the Army Colt from the holster on his belt.

"At 'em, Jimmie!" Mort yelled, thumb cocking the revolver and bounding forward.

Needing no urging, Thatcher raced towards the clearing by the side of his companion. He saw the remaining Indians were registering consternation at the intervention, but they showed no sign of taking flight. Instead, they began to raise their muzzle loading carbines. Antiquated and firing only a single shot although these undoubtedly were, they would prove deadly at close quarters. Therefore, his sister was still far from out of danger.

Regardless of what his companions meant to do, although one was the favorite son of a senior Waco war chief, Corovan had no intention of helping them. He was too aware of how competently Mort Lewis could fight and equally cognizant of the fact that the young men he had persuaded to leave the reservation on a raiding mission were inexperienced as warriors. With that in mind, feeling sure he of all of them could expect no mercy at the hands of the guide, he had no desire to remain and face the consequences. For a moment, being a sufficiently expert rider to require neither saddle nor bridle, he thought of speeding his departure by using one of the horses in the clearing. Then he remembered they were hobbled and incapable of hurried movement. What was more, from the position he was now standing in, he could see each had the letters, VL, burned into its rump. The brand meant they belonged to Mort Lewis and, as demanded by his Comanche upbringing, he would remorselessly hunt down anybody who stole even one of them.

Spinning upon his heel, paying not the slightest attention to the brave struggling to escape from the jaws of the big dog, Corovan saw from the corner of his eye the lance carrier being shot. Realizing the father of the would be warrior was going to be furious on learning what had happened, he knew the only way in which he could return to the lucrative Waco reservation was to be able to announce he had taken revenge upon the killer. Despite this appreciation of the situation, he had no intention of trying to take vengeance immediately. Running the kind of risks involved by such an undertaking had never been his way.

Thinking only of saving his own skin, shelving the matter of revenge until this could be attained without danger to himself, Corovan sprinted in the direction from which he had come as fast as his legs could carry him. Nor, despite hearing shots from various firearms to his rear, did he look back. Instead, he returned through the bushes to where he and his companions had left their mounts when moving in to learn whose tracks they had been following.

Alarmed by what was happening, Geraldine could not prevent herself from taking an involuntary pace to the rear. However, doing so saved her life. Catching her heel against the saddle upon which she had sat while drawing, she toppled backwards. The providential accident was only just in time.

Of the three young braves armed with the carbines, only one had already cocked the action. Being aware that they were far from proficient in using the weapons and wanting to reduce the chance of a premature discharge, Corovan had ordered them not to cock the action before commencing the stalking on foot. However, while his companions had been too absorbed in studying the girl and horses to think of it, the exception had drawn back the hammer before entering the clearing.

Showing himself more skillful in other aspects too, the brave had his carbine in the firing position while his companions were still cocking their pieces. As he could not see the men amongst the bushes, he sighted at the girl. Just as he had squeezed the trigger to the point where the sear released the hammer, he saw his intended victim starting to disappear from view. This would not have had any effect if he was using a modern, metal cartridge firearm. The action of the old, percussion fired, 'trade gun' was slower.

By the time the hammer swung forward to strike the copper cap, sending a spurt of flame to ignite the powder charge in the chamber, she had fallen just far enough for the discharged bullet to pass close above her.

Seeing what was happening as they burst into the clearing, Mort and Thatcher were only moderately relieved!

While Geraldine had avoided being shot by the brave, her perils were still far from at an end!

Having made their carbines ready for use, the other two Indians were starting to take aim at the girl. Ignoring what they were doing in his eagerness to count coup on her, the third did not offer to reload. Instead, swinging up the weapon with the intention of using its butt as an extemporized club, he bounded towards where she had fallen.

CHAPTER SIX

One You Call Friend is Enemy

Guided by habits acquired through having ridden horses for most of her life and taken her fair share of falls, Geraldine Thatcher sought instinctively to reduce the impact from the unexpected tumble. Aided by the springy turf upon which she arrived, she contrived to land without more than receiving a jolt. Apart from being slightly winded, she was otherwise in possession of all her faculties and retained her hold on the Colt Navy Model of 1853 revolver. Looking up, despite realizing her brother and Morton Lewis must be close by, she discovered that she might still have need of the weapon to protect herself. Already the Indian who had tried to shoot her was approaching to continue the assault.

Sprawled supine, the girl reacted to the threat. Thrusting the revolver upwards, an instinct for self preservation directing her thumb to cock the hammer, she pointed and fired it. However, although she hit her intended assailant in the right side, the light powder charge and comparatively small size of the .36 caliber conical bullet lacked sufficient "stopping" power to halt, or even turn him aside. Instead, he began to bound over the saddle upon which she had tripped and it seemed certain that he would either alight upon her, or would be close enough to smash home the butt of his carbine.

Skidding to a halt a few feet from the fringe of the bushes, although First Lieutenant James Thatcher ran onwards, Mort Lewis took in the situation and drew his conclusions with great rapidity. The two young Waco braves who had not yet fired their carbines were preparing to do so. If he and his companion devoted attention to them, the third was at liberty to complete his attack upon the girl. Yet, to shoot this buck and rely upon the officer to deal with another would still leave the third to take her life.

"Pete!" the guide bellowed, selecting what he considered to be the only course for his party. "Drop it!"

Even as it heard its master's voice, the big dog had grown aware that the man it attacked had ceased to struggle. Therefore, it was able to obey the command immediately. Opening its jaws to free the throat, from which blood spurted out of gashes ripped as far as the windpipe by its teeth, it looked around. At the sight of the brave who had fired rushing by, it swung from its victim and darted in his direction.

Once again, Pete arrived in time to prevent Geraldine from being attacked!

Having gained momentum, the dog rose into the air upon converging course with the brave. He was at the apex of his bound over the saddle when the ninety pounds of hard muscled animal reached and struck him. Closing with a crushing pressure, yet only a slight burning sensation as the teeth sank through the sleeve of his jacket and into his flesh,[1] the jaws grasped his raised right forearm. The shock of the unexpected attack, combined with the weight of the dog, knocked him sideways and they went down together well clear of the girl.

Relieved by Pete of the most pressing threat to Geraldine's well being, Mort was able to give thought to dealing with the others. In one respect, his shout to the dog was already playing its part in doing so. Hearing him, the surviving pair of braves had become aware of the hazard posed by the arrival of Thatcher and himself in the clearing. Realizing they posed a far graver danger than either the girl or the dog, the bucks began to turn the barrels of the carbines in their direction. Nor, despite the comparative inexperience in handling of the users, was Mort and Thatcher's position

1. *The author can state from personal experience this was the sensation he felt on those occasions during his twelve and a half years service with the Royal Army Veterinary Corps when he was bitten by a guard dog. The pain comes later. J.T.E.*

any more of a sinecure than rescuing the girl had been. At the distance separating them, the 'trade guns' of the Indians had an advantage in range over their Colt 1860 Army revolvers which might prove the decisive factor.

Bringing up the Colt, his left hand going to join and help the right hold it more steadily, the guide aimed via the notch at the tip of the hammer which served as a backsight when fully cocked. Covering the brave who was swinging the carbine towards him, he squeezed the trigger. Rudimentary though the sighting arrangements of the revolver undoubtedly were, they proved adequate for his purpose. Flying as he had intended, the .44 caliber soft lead ball caught the brave in the center of the forehead. Although killed instantly, a spasmodic jerk of the right forefinger discharged the weapon. However, its barrel had been tilted out of alignment and the bullet flew harmlessly into the air.

Filled with fear for the life of his sister though Thatcher might be, he nevertheless contrived to keep sufficient control over his emotions to behave in a sensible fashion. Although he fired twice on the run, being just as aware as the guide of his revolver's limitations, he was not acting on blind impulse. Instead, he was seeking to divert the attention of the braves from Geraldine to himself. He was partially successful in this. Hearing the crack of the Army Colt, the taller of the survivors looked towards him and began to direct the carbine his way.

Throwing himself forward, the lieutenant landed stomach down on the ground. Resting his elbows, he too adopted a double handed hold to allow improved accuracy. As had been the case when stalking the buffalo, he had had sufficient on his mind to distract it from the throbbing ache emitted by his right shoulder. The jolt caused by his landing brought the pain to the fore again. Trying to control it, he touched off a shot. Instantly, his instinct for such matters warned he would not make the required hit. Nor, as he saw through the swirl of white gaseous 'smoke' which followed the bullet from the muzzle, had he done so.

Able to see and understand the dilemma of his companion, Mort cocked the Colt as it rose on the recoil. Bringing down the barrel, he swivelled at the waist and fired with both hands still on the butt. While he made a hit, despite the speed with which he acted, it produced a less lethal effect than his previous effort. Not that he had any cause to regret his failure to take a longer and more careful aim.

Raked across the bent left forearm by the bullet, a yelp of pain burst from the brave. The carbine flew from his grasp an instant before he was ready to fire at Thatcher. Seeing he alone of his war party was on his feet, he concluded there was nothing further he could do against the white-eye ride-plenties[2] who had proved as competent warriors as he had always heard was the case with their kind. With that thought in mind, he clasped the grazed limb with his right hand and fled across the clearing in the direction already taken by "Dead Face," as his people and other Indians named Dennis "Waxie" Corovan.

Satisfied the young brave posed no further threat to Geraldine and themselves, Mort and Thatcher were content to let him go. However, glancing around the clearing, the guide realized there was one disadvantage to showing such clemency. An instant later, the lieutenant—having conducted a similar scrutiny—referred to the reason for his misgivings.

"Where's Corovan?" Thatcher asked, starting to rise.

"Took a greaser standoff," Mort replied, employing the term for running away used by Texas' cowhands. "And if I send Pete after him, that fool ole dog's like to pull down the buck instead."

"It doesn't matter whether he gets away," the lieutenant declared, walking to where his sister was sitting up. "We can both identify him and I'll see to it that a warrant is issued for his arrest. This time, we can *prove* he's been up to something illegal. Are you all right, Gerrie?"

"Y—Yes!" the girl answered, looking about her and clearly struggling to retain control of her emotions. "You came back just in time!"

"Come away, you fool critter!" the guide commanded,

---

2. *"Ride-plenty"*: *Indians' name for a Texas cowhand, given as a sign of respect for the ability they shared with the braves as horsemen. J.T.E.*

seeing the second brave tackled by Pete had either been stunned by the fall or had fainted and was offering no resistance. "He's all through."

Even as Mort was speaking, there came the sound of rapidly approaching hooves from amongst the bushes. Swinging around and seeing that the commotion was caused by swiftly riding Indians, the lieutenant gave a startled growl and started to raise his Colt-filled left hand.

"Don't need that, Jimmie!" Mort claimed, his voice for once sounding relieved rather than unemotional. "They're *Kweharehnuh!*"

Dashing into the clearing at a gallop, half a dozen Indians brought their fast moving ponies to a halt in a rough half circle around the girl and two men with the panache of extremely competent riders. Although not all were armed in such a fashion, the rifles and carbines which some carried were of a later and better quality than the "trade guns" of the young Wacos. What was more, although the girl was in no condition to appreciate the point at that moment, their appearance was equally superior. None of them wore clothing discarded by white men. Indicative of a people who spent their lives on the open plains where such animals were still plentiful, the majority of their leatherwork—including a square of rawhide suspended on the shoulders which could be held over the head as protection against the sun, giving their band an alternative name, *Kwahihekehnuh*, "Sunshades On Their Backs"—was made from the skins of pronghorns.

"Proud-Son-Of-Two-People!" greeted the foremost rider, his eagle feather headdress—called a "war bonnet" by some people—and the lance he carried indicating he was a warrior of consequence. In addition to employing the man-name granted by the *Kweharehnuh* to Mort, there was a warm smile on his badly scarred yet handsome and noble features as he continue, "Healing Hands said you were come to hunt our land, brother, so we rode to join you."

"My heart is always glad to see you, *Cicatriz Honorable*," the guide answered, speaking the Antelope dialect of the *Nemenuh* as fluently as the warrior who had addressed him and showing no surprise at being informed that the respected senior medicine man of the band had possessed such information about him. He was aware that such people had powers which were beyond the comprehension of those outside their own circle. Glancing at the sprawled figures of the Waco braves, he went on grimly, "Dead Face brought these *tuivitsi* to raid on our land, but ran away and left them when they fought. Can you send your brothers after him?"

"I could," the lance carrier replied. "But it is said a *Wawai* never rides faster and better than when he is being chased and our horses have been ridden hard."

"Then let the *Namae'enuh* go, brother," Mort decided, using another and less polite title for the Comanche band which supplied half of Corovan's birthright. [3] "His life is not worth that of a warrior's horse and I can settle accounts with him later." While speaking, he had turned his gaze to the rest of the men with Noble Scar and noticed the youngest of them was carrying, in addition to a bow and arrows, the Sharps New Model of 1866 rifle belonging to Thatcher. Although he knew this was not the case, he continued, "My thanks for bringing that for me, *brave-heart!*"

"I found it and that makes it *mine!*" the youngster asserted truculently and, although the term was unknown amongst his people, his demeanor implied an addition of, "So *there!*" as he eyed such an item as he had hoped-but never expected-to come by. Then he glared defiantly at the speaker.

"It belongs to my friend here," the guide stated with an equal air of irrevocability, twirling into its holster the revolver he was holding and gesturing to Thatcher who had already done so. "He is my guest, *tuivitsi*, and left it behind deliberately when we came to rescue his sister, so you can hand it over *now* and I thank you for fetching it to him."

While delivering the second part of his speech, Mort signalled for the dog to remain where it was, and he started to walk towards the brave he was addressing. Despite his leisurely seeming gait, his bearing conveyed an aura of menace and determination. Wise in such matters, he judged

3. "Namae'enuh": *put politely, "They who have incestuous intercourse"* J.T.E.

the youngster to be no more experienced that the Wacos had been, although he was equally desirous of making it appear otherwise. As was generally the case with such a person, no matter what his race, any show of hesitancy in enforcing the request would be construed as a sign of weakness and inferior status.

There was, however, another reason for Mort adopting such a stand on the issue. The streak of pride which would not allow him to back off in the face of provocation at Holbrock, when to have done so could have been considered diplomatic where his relationship with the citizens was concerned, was also causing him to face up to what he knew to be a challenge now. No *tehnap*, which he could claim to be amongst members of both sides of his birthright, would ever accept such behavior from a *tuivitsi* and he knew he would lose face in the eyes of the other braves should he do so. What was more, it would reflect adversely upon his maternal grandfather. He had no intention of permitting such a thing to happen, nor would he be expected to.

Watching the tall figure stalking towards him, the young brave began to experience a twinge of apprehension. He had heard that Proud-Son-Of-Two People was a name-warrior and here he was presented with evidence to support the claim. It was obvious that some of the Wacos had fallen to the grandson of Wolf Runner and the youngster was all too aware that he still had to count coup upon an enemy himself. However, while he wished to retain so valuable and desirable a piece of property, he realized this would only be possible if he defied the older and vastly more experienced warrior. Every instinct he possessed warned this would prove dangerous and painful. He also knew the other members of his party would have no sympathy for him regardless of what happened. On the other hand, they would understand and think no worse of him if he yielded before a brave-heart of such known superior standing.

"Here!" the youngster said, trying to look more pleasant than he was feeling. "My father has ridden many war trails with Wolf Runner, so I give you this for your friend, Proud-Son-Of-Two-People."

"My thanks, warrior," Mort answered, accepting the rifle and wanting to do all he could to minimize the humiliation he knew the other was experiencing. "Tell your father from me that he has trained his son well."

At that moment, there was an interruption which was welcomed by the youngster.

Groaning, the brave who had been wounded by Geraldine and suffered the attack from the big dog sat up. Gazing about him in a frightened fashion, he felt at each of his injuries in turn. Taking their attention from Mort and the tuivitsi, the girl and all the men looked his way.

"Why did you come here?" *Cicatriz Honorable* demanded, jumping from his horse and striding to confront the alarmed Waco.

"Dead Face brought us to ask for brave-hearts to share a war trail with us," the injured brave replied, trying to prevent his feelings from being observed by the *Kweharehnuh*. "On our way to find your village, we came upon tracks of horses with iron feet and followed. When we found the woman with them, we though to take her and them."

"You saw *that?*" Noble Scar barked, pointing with his Winchester Model of 1866 carbine to where the medicine pouch was still lying across the seat of Mort's saddle.

"Y-Yes!" the Waco admitted worriedly.

"You know what it is?" the *Kweharehnuh* leader challenged.

"Yes," the wounded brave confessed. "But Dead Face told us it must have been taken from its dead owner by the white-eyes and meant nothing."

"Dead Face lied!" Noble Scar stated. "Are any of you *known?*"

"Brave Rider is son of Chief Kills Plenty Pawnee," the Waco replied, aware of what was meant and indicating with his blood covered right hand the brave who had carried the war lance.

"The chief is known to me," *Cicatriz Honorable* declared. "We will care for your injuries, then you will go back to tell him what has happened. Say Proud-Son-Of-Two People, grandson of Chief Wolf Runner was not at fault and the blame for these deaths is that of Dead Face."

"That I will do!" the Waco promised, relieved to discover he was to be let off so lightly after what he had been a party to.

"See you do!" Noble Scar commanded and, having given an order for the treatment of the injuries, he turned to Mort. "Do you come to our village, brother?"

"It has been long since last I greeted my *tawk,*" the guide replied, using the Comanche word meaning "grandfather" or "grandson" depending upon who was saying it. "Besides, my friend has need of help from Healing Hands."

"Are you getting the pictures you want, ma'am?" Mort Lewis inquired, going to where Geraldine Thatcher was sitting upon the stump of a tree and holding the open drawing case in her hands.

After the injuries of the wounded Waco had been treated, and the horses belonging to his dead companions had been collected, he was given their weapons and allowed to leave. Despite the danger to which she had been subjected by him, the girl had expressed concern over this being permitted. On having her comments translated by Mort, Noble Scar had stated he had brought the misfortunes upon himself and, if he wished to be considered a brave-heart, must accept the suffering while returning to his people.

At the request of the guide, while a couple of the *Kwe-harehnuh* were ascertaining that Waxie Corovan was not lurking anywhere in the vicinity, the others had helped him skin and remove the head from the buffalo bull. With these tasks completed, he and his two companions were escorted to the chuckwagon by the braves. Giving his cook and the striker the instructions he had outlined to Lieutenant Thatcher, he had found them subjected to revision. As she had on other occasions, the girl had asked to accompany her brother and Mort. Granted permission, even though she was un-aware that the pace had been slowed down for her benefit, she had had the hardest ride of her life before arriving at their destination.

Despite the lateness of the hour, Geraldine and her brother

had received a cordial welcome from Chief Wolf Runner as friends of his grandson. They had had an unoccupied buffalo hide *tipi* placed at their disposal and, tired by the journey, both had slept as soundly as if in their own beds at home. Waking late in the morning, the girl had discovered she was alone. On looking out of the flaps which served as a door, she had found Mort and his grandfather waiting by a fire not far away. Told that her brother had been taken to allow the medicine man to attend to his badly bruised right shoulder, she was asked how she would like to spend her time.

The treatment of the lieutenant's injury had required longer than Mort anticipated. However, he had stated there was still sufficient time for the Thatchers to catch the stagecoach which would return them to Fort Bracken. Accepting his judgement, Geraldine had set about making the most of her stay. Not only had it allowed her to make sketches of various activities around the village, but she was given an insight to the way in which many Indians had lived prior to being placed upon reservations.

Having spent a second night in the village, being guests at a dance organized for her benefit by Wolf Runner and the "old man" chiefs, the girl had decided how she might repay the kindness and consideration shown to herself and her brother. She had, in fact, just completed the gift for her host when his grandson came up and spoke to her.

"Yes, thank you," Geraldine replied, face flushed with pleasure, holding forward the open case. "Do you think Wolf Runner will like this reminder of our visit?"

"By cracky, won't he though?" Mort declared, looking at a very lifelike drawing depicting himself, his grandfather and Thatcher standing outside a *tipi*. "You've got us all down there clear's one of them tintype pictures I've seen, even to Grandpappy Wolf Runner's best clothes and the patterning of the brass studs on his 'old yellowboy' rifle.[4] This's choicely good, ma'am."

"I'm pleased you like it," the girl said, delighted by the

---

4. *"Old yellowboy": name given to the Winchester Model of 1866 rifle, on account of its frame being made from brass. J.T.E.*

genuine praise. "Let me sign it and put on the date, then we'll give it to your grandfather."

"He'll certain sure treasure it, ma'am," the guide stated, then nodded to where Thatcher was approaching accompanied by an elderly *Kweharehnuh* who limped badly. "Here comes Jimmie and Healing Hands. How's the shoulder, *amigo?*"

"Working as good as ever," the lieutenant answered, swinging his right arm with complete ease and freedom of movement. "Will you thank Healing Hands for me, please?"

"It was a small thing," asserted the stocky, grey-haired and gentle faced medicine man. "But you, Proud-Son-Of-Two-People, take care. One you call friend is enemy."

"Who would that be, wise old one?" Mort asked.

"He is not of the *Nemenuh*," Healing Hands replied. "So be on your guard when you go back amongst your father's people."

"I will remember your words," the guide promised, having too much respect for the powers possessed by a medicine man of the quality of his informant to discount what he had been told, even though he could not imagine what had provoked the warning.

Thinking over Healing Hands' words, Mort was unable to decide to whom they might apply. This was because—as he was to discover later—although they were acquaintances, he had never considered the person to whom the medicine man was referring as being a friend.

CHAPTER SEVEN

You'll Have to Kill Him

"Good evening, *Mr.* Corovan, if that's what you're still calling yourself," David Masefield Stewart greeted, displaying no suggestion of cordiality and welcome, as he ran a far from amiable gaze over the man brought into the room he referred to as his study by his butler. "Mr. Scanlan and I were wondering why you've been showing so much interest in my affairs since you hit Holbrock."

Everything about the owner of what was now the biggest ranch in Holbrock County indicated that, even if not born to it, he enjoyed luxury and was willing to go to considerable expense to ensure that he lived in suitable surroundings. Although his hired hands had to be satisfied with far less elegant and comfortable quarters, even though they were not so bad as rumor claimed were supplied by "cattle king" John Chisum,[1] the ranch house itself was built after the style popular amongst the wealthy *hacienderos* in Mexico. He was served by a domestic staff which would not have been out of place at a major mansion in Austin. Nor would its furnishings and fittings have disgraced such a setting in the capital city of Texas. Leatherbound volumes lined the walls of the "study," interspersed by costly paintings. In its center, the main item of furniture was a massive and well polished desk.

1. *According to the legend, having promised his hired hands better accommodation on moving into superior quarters himself, John Chisum showed them into an adobe shack which had as its sole furnishings a bottle of whiskey in each corner and another in the middle of its dirt floor. J.T.E.*

About five foot nine inches in height, Stewart was a thickset man in his late forties. While bulky and obviously fond of good living, he still gave the impression of having solid flesh rather than flabby fat. Closely cropped, his black hair was turning grey at the temples and becoming thin on top. Clean shaven, despite the dark blue tinge to his jaws suggesting otherwise, his face was tanned and, at that moment, there were lines of uncompromising hardness under its apparent benevolence. He was wearing a dark red velvet smoking jacket over an open necked white silk shirt. However, although the time was just after ten o'clock at night, his black trousers were tucked into the Hessian legs of brown riding boots. A heavy plaited leather quirt lay on the desk close to his right hand, but he gave no sign of being armed in any way. In fact, he always took great care to establish that he never carried a gun.

Being unarmed was unlikely to produce repercussions, regardless of his unfriendly attitude towards the man he had had brought to see him, as the rancher was not alone in the study.

"Cousin Slats and Salar weren't so drunk they didn't know you was pumping them last night," the other occupant of the study asserted. "So Mr. Stewart passed the word to have you fetched out here should you try it on with any of the other boys tonight."

Lounging at the right side of the desk, occupying a chair deliberately selected as being somewhat smaller and not quite so comfortable as the one used by his employer, Wilson "Leftie" Scanlan was subjecting the visitor to an equally disdainful scrutiny while speaking. Just past thirty, black haired, tall, lean and wiry, with a heavily moustached face which seemed carved from old leather, he was segundo of the Standing DMS—the letters being positioned one above another on the branding iron—ranch. His tidy and expensive cowhand style clothing notwithstanding, he was just as much a "warrior" as any other member of the crew and more competent than the rest. Before starting to work for Stewart, he had acquired a reputation for earning a very good living by the skill with which he could handle the brace of ivory handled Remington New Army Model of 1863 revolvers in the fast draw holsters of his *buscadero* gunbelt.

"Well," the rancher said, his accent New England. "What's it all about?"

"Mort Lewis," replied Dennis "Waxie" Corovan, having changed his clothes for those of the no more cleanly attire of a professional gambler. He showed no sign of being put out, either in having been compelled to come to the ranch house, or in the less than friendly attitudes of the two men confronting him.

"What about Mort Lewis?" Stewart demanded.

"You're wanting his spread," the renegade stated. "And old Dexter Chass's place."

"Now what makes you think a thing like that?" Stewart asked, sounding disinterested in spite of the glance he exchanged with his segundo.

"Big rancher like you allus needs to grow bigger," Corovan explained. "Your range's already holding all the stock it can take without you getting more water, and you can only get that hereabouts by taking over the VL and Chass's Hanging C. Trouble being, ain't neither of 'em likely to sell out no matter how much good cash money you put up afore 'em."

"Go on," the rancher prompted, without offering to either confirm or deny what he was being told.

"What I know about Mort Lewis," the renegade obliged. "You'll have to kill him afore you'll get his spread. Same'll apply to that ornery ole son-of-a-bitch, Dex Chass, 'cepting he'll be some easier than that part-*Kweharehnuh* god damned half breed to take out."

"And you figure you can kill Mort Lewis for me?" Stewart suggested dryly, the words being echoed by a derisive sniff from Scanlan."

"Hell, *no!*" Corovan denied emphatically. "I know I'm not nowheres near's good's some of your boys, much less Leftie here. So I couldn't take him out in what'd pass as a fair fight. Which, with a feller like Jerome Dickson being sheriff and Lewis having so many *bueno amigos* among the officers of the Second Cavalry, you'd need to have it made look that way. Wasn't for needing that, you'd've had him made wolf bait long afore now."

"I'm not admitting *anything,* one way or another, mind," Stewart warned, concluding his unkempt and unprepossessing visitor was more shrewd than appeared on the surface. "But you've got something more on your mind than just telling me that."

"Sure," Corovan admitted. "I've come up with a way you can have both of them took out, so's it'll look like Mort Lewis got put under all legal and proper—Or, at least, so's it won't look like you personal had nothing to do with him getting made wolf bait."

"And how much is it going to cost me?" the rancher inquired, as the renegade stopped speaking with the air of one who had much more to offer.

"I reckon we can settle on what you'll call a fair price," Corovan replied.

"I *always* pay a fair price," Stewart claimed. "But I've got to be given my money's worth before I hand it over."

"I reckon you'll figure you've got *that,*" the renegade stated.

"Then let's hear what you have so I can decide on it," the rancher commanded.

"Run across Lewis taking a dude and gal hunting in the *Kweharehnuh* country," Corovan said, being too wise to try to discuss terms of payment first and sticking to what was basically the truth. "I reckon you knowed he was doing it?"

"I knew," Stewart confirmed non-committally.

"Seemed the dude'd hurt his arm some way," Corovan continued. "So Lewis's took him to let the medicine man at the Antelope village 'tend his hurt. Just then, he sent his chuck wagon off and's likely figuring to catch it up at Sanchez Riley's, or somewhere else along the way. Whichever, they'll call by at Riley's and I've fixed it so he'll be give word that ole Dex Chass's causing fuss on his land when he gets there. 'Less I'm mistook about him, he'll be headed here as fast's that big claybank gelding of his can tote him."

"And how does that help *me?*" the rancher asked, glancing at the calender on his desk and estimating how much time remained of Morton Lewis's hunting trip.

"Suppose he found his place burned down and those two hands of his'n dead when he got there," the renegade replied. "With signs leading straight to the Hanging C?"

"He'd go on over with head down and horns a-hooking," Scanlan guessed, also concluding his employer was finding what was said by Corovan interesting. "Which'd see to ole Chass and his son, but neither of them are close to good enough to take him 'long of them comes gun play."

"And nobody would blame him for going after them, the reason he could give," Stewart supplemented.

"There's some in Holbrock'd want to lay blame," Corovan contradicted. "Like that fancy-talking, lard-gutted banker, Humboldt. Way I heard it, he's not over-tooken with the notion of a half breed wanting to be his son-in-law and'd be the first to start pushing for what he'd call getting justice done."

"Humboldt's a real big man in Holbrock," the rancher conceded pensively and with just a trace of animosity. "But Jerome Dickson isn't under his thumb, or anybody else's. Comes what may, he'll go by the way the evidence shows it happened."

"Even Dickson won't be able to call it self defense should Dex Chass 'n' his boy be found shot in the back," Corovan pointed out. "And, should he bring Lewis in for trial, I reckon there'll be those who'll start yelling 'hang-rope' 'stead of waiting for it."

"Dickson would stop anybody who tried lynching a man he was holding prisoner," Stewart stated. "I know him well enough to be sure of that."

"Likely, only I've heard tell of sheriff's got killed trying to stop a lynching," the renegade countered, looking pointedly from the rancher to his segundo and back. "Which, should it happen, I don't figure there'd be all too fired much trouble finding *somebody* to take his place."

"Aren't you forgetting something *real* important?" Stewart challenged, having no intention of admitting he would be only too willing to have his segundo—or another more compliant, peace officer—appointed sheriff of Holbrock County.

"What'd that be?" Corovan asked, genuinely puzzled.

"Wolf Runner!" the rancher said coldly. "From what I've told, he feels real strongly about his grandson and is certain to come looking for revenge on whoever had Lewis killed."

"That'll be the folks in town, not *you*," the renegade replied, deciding he was up against a much more shrewd man than he had envisaged. "Lewis reckons you're his *amigo*, so it'll be them's Wolf Runner goes after, not you. Which being, the folks's come through it aren't likely to show too much grief, nor kind thoughts, about Lewis seeing's what his granddaddy's done to them."

"You've put some thought into this," Stewart commended dryly. "So what's Lewis done to you?"

"He got my brother 'n' some good *amigos* killed by those Yankee blue bellies' he rode scout for," the renegade answered, which again was true as far as it went. He did not explain how he had only just escaped with his life, or how the activities he and the victims were engaged upon warranted the stringent measures taken against them. "And I'm a man who allus looks for evens."

"'Specially should you figure to get somebody else to do it for you," the segundo put in, eyeing the visitor with cold contempt. "And look to make money out of it at the same time."

"There's no call for that attitude, Mr. Scanlan," Stewart declared, with what might have been reproof. His tone became gentler as he went on, "You've made some real good sense, Mr. Corovan, but I'll need time to think about it. Have you eaten?"

"Not recent," the renegade lied, never being one to miss the chance of obtaining a free meal.

"Then tell my butler to take you to the kitchen and see what the cook can find for you," the rancher authorized. "By the time you're through, I'll have decided whether to do what you suggest—and how much you deserve for doing it."

"A man couldn't ask for no more than that," Corovan declared, exuding blatant sycophancy. "I know I can count on you to do right by me."

"There's a whole heap to what he says, boss," Scanlan claimed, after the renegade had left the study.

"He's got the basic idea, all right," Stewart admitted. "But there's a better way to make it happen. I'm leaving for Austin in the morning and this is what I want you to have done."

Although the rancher was convinced he would be able to use Corovan for his own ends, as he was giving the instructions to his segundo, he failed to realize that by adopting even his revised version of the scheme he was being manipulated. While he had guessed correctly what the response would be from Wolf Runner to the killing of Mort Lewis, neither he nor Scanlan possessed sufficient knowledge to appreciate all the ramifications. Being far better informed, the renegade was aware that the news of what happened would encourage restless braves of the other Comanche bands and various nations to quit the reservations and ride similar war trails. When this happened, he was confident he could earn a far greater sum of money than he was likely to receive from Stewart.

The Ysabel Kid woke up knowing he had just received a message. Yet, had he felt the need to look, he would have discovered only he of the fifteen men who were sleeping around the camp fire had been disturbed. Originating from something over a quarter of a mile away, he could hear not only the few movements of the three thousand or so head of longhorn cattle which constituted the bedded down trail herd of the OD Connected ranch but also the slowly stepping hooves of the horses ridden by whichever pair of cowhands were keeping watch over them. Closer at hand, the night hawk was performing a similar duty with the at present unused mounts in the *remuda*.[2] Apart from them, nobody else was awake. Not even the night horses for the rest of the crew, which were sleeping on their feet saddled and ready for use along the picket line between the chuck and bed wagons.

Nor had the Kid expected to find otherwise!

While he had been informed where to go, and that his presence was required urgently on a matter of great importance, the Kid was aware the message was not delivered verbally. Nor had it come by any conventional means. It had been sent to him with the aid of what the people of his maternal grandfather called "medicine."

Despite having been raised as a *Pehnane* Comanche, attaining the status of a fully fledged warrior in the band's Dog Soldier war lodge,[3] the only knowledge the Kid had of "medicine" was that it worked!

Every member of the *Nemenuh* accepted "medicine" as a proven fact, but its secrets were the sole province of those select few who had been initiated into its age-old mysteries. Invariably, although a younger person who lacked the qualities necessary to become a warrior could start to acquire the knowledge, the medicine men were mostly older people. Having won the man-name, *Cuchilo*—the Knife—by virture of his superlative skill at wielding one and through his general competence in the fighting line, the Kid most certainly had not come into such a pacific category. Rather the

2. *Although a wrangler was employed to look after the horses of a trail drive's* remuda *during the hours of daylight, a "night hawk" was hired to perform this task while the rest of the crew, excepting those hands riding "night herd" on the cattle, were asleep. J.T.E.*

3. *Details regarding the family background and special qualifications of the Ysabel Kid, also an explanation of various Comanche terms can be found in:* APPENDIX TWO. *J.T.E.*

opposite, in fact. However, despite having spent the majority of his life among white folks, this was not the first occasion he had been brought into contact with and profited from the mysterious powers of "medicine."[4]

Sitting up, the Kid flipped open the upper half of the seven by eighteen feet of waterproofed Number 8 white "ducking" tarpaulin which had been wrapped around his bedding and shoved away the blanket and thick suggan quilt. He came to his feet in a lithe movement, but did not reach for the low heeled black riding boots standing near his bed. Instead, after taking a swift glance around, he opened the neck of the warbag he had been using as a pillow. Taking out the pair of Comanche moccasins which were the uppermost items, he donned them. However, although his Winchester Model of 1866 rifle and black leather gunbelt—with a Colt Second Model Dragon revolver butt forward in the low cavalry twist draw holster on the right and a massive ivory handled James Black bowie knife sheathed at the left—were within reaching distance, he did not attempt to take up any of them.

About six foot in height, the Kid had a slender build which was anything but puny. Rather it was suggestive of a wiry and tireless strength, a speed of movement and an agility well beyond average. His hair, black as a raven's wing was more wavy than that of a pure Comanche, indicative of the white side of his birthright. Indian dark and seeming younger than his actual age, his handsome features appeared to express an almost babyish innocence in repose. However, when danger threatened, or in moments of stress, they could become more in keeping with the red hazel eyes which alone gave a warning of his true nature in times of peace. Like the boots—their low heels a sign that his duties might require more walking than would those of a cowhand—and gunbelt, his tight rolled bandana, open necked shirt, trousers and the low crowned, wide brimmed hat

---

4. *Two occasions when the Ysabel Kid benefited from "medicine" are recorded in:* COMANCHE *and* GO BACK TO HELL. *J.T.E.*

swinging by its *barbiquejo* chinstrap from the horn of his saddle were all black.

"Dusty!" the Kid said, stepping to the nearest sleeping shape on his right.

Quietly though the word was spoken, the man to whom it had been addressed woke instantly. Even sitting up, it was obvious he was not tall. Beyond him, a much larger figure stirred and rose from its bed.

"Yes?" asked Captain Dustine Edward Marsden "Dusty" Fog.

Although the trail boss and segundo of the great OD Connected ranch,[5] the speaker was young and not more than five foot inches in height. For all that, there was a width to his shoulders, tapering to a lean waist and powerful legs, suggestive of strength beyond average. Yet, expensive though they were, he contrived to make his cowhand style clothing look like the cast offs of a much better favored person and they tended to detract from his appearance. Under shortish dusty blond hair, tanned by the elements, his face was handsome without being eye-catching. There was, nevertheless, an intelligence and power in its lines if one took the trouble to look. Something in his grey eyes and mouth, which smiled easily, would inform the discerning he had the undefinable presence of a born leader regardless of his size or age.

"I've just got word from Raccoon Talker," the Kid announced, squatting on his heels alongside the small Texan and holding his pleasant tenor drawl low to avoid disturbing the rest of the trail crew. "She's wanting me to help."

"Where is she?" Dusty inquired, his voice equally indicative of origins in the Lone Star State, although he had had a better formal education.

The small Texan knew the person to whom his companion was referring to be the senior medicine woman of the *Pehn-*

---

5. *The family background and special qualifications of Captain Dustine Edward Marsden 'Dusty' Fog are recorded in:* APPENDIX ONE. *J.T.E.*

ane Comanche, but he was equally aware that she was unlikely to be in the immediate vicinity of the trail herd. For all that, he had no need to be told how she was able to deliver the message. He had often heard of the mysterious powers possessed by Indian medicine men and women. What was more, he realized the matter must be one of especial urgency and importance for Raccoon Talker to have used her "medicine" techniques to contact his black dressed *amigo*.

"On the reservation," the Kid replied.

"Does she need you to go there?"

"Nope. Allows there could come bad trouble in the *Kweharehnuh* country and you 'n' me're the best suited to stop it."

"The *Kweharehnuh,* huh?"

"Wolf Runner's village," the Kid elaborated. "Happen I recall it right, they range some south of the main band."

"That would be down Holbrock County way, wouldn't it?" Dusty guessed.

"Thereabout."

"Well I'll be damned," the small Texan breathed. "If you read something like it in a book, you'd never believe it. Uncle Devil told me to call at Holbrock on the way back from delivering the herd to Fort Sumner and look in on a feller who's put up a business deal to him."

"This won't wait until we've done that," the Kid warned.

"Best see it doesn't have to then," the small Texan replied and looked at the exceptionally handsome, golden blond haired young giant who was listening to the conversation. "Take the herd, Mark and, happen you haven't heard anything from me before, head up to Holbrock with the boys when you're through."

"You figure it'll come bad enough to need us, Lon?" Mark Counter asked.[6]

6. *Information regarding the family background and special qualifications of Mark Counter can be found in various volumes of the* Floating Outfit *series. J.T.E.*

"If it isn't bad enough, Raccoon Talker calling me that way, it'll do 'til something bad comes around," the Kid answered somberly. "I'm just hoping Dusty and me can get there in time to take cards."

CHAPTER EIGHT

Arrest Him for Murder

"Well I'll be damned!" Sheriff Jerome Dickson ejaculated, lifting his gaze from the report he was writing at his desk to find out who had entered his office. "I was figuring on coming to look for you when I'd finished this."

The senior peace officer of Holbrock County was a tall, lean man in his early forties. Tanned, strong, his face had a neatly trimmed reddish-brown moustache which gave a firm set to his lips. Although he was wearing a white collarless shirt, the trousers and vest of a brown suit—with its jacket hanging over the back of his chair—and Hersome gaiter boots, there was much in his posture to indicate he had served for several years as an officer in the United States' Cavalry. His gunbelt, a walnut handled Colt 1860 Army revolver in its fast draw holster, lay on the desk within easy reach of his right hand. However, despite having discovered the identity of his visitor and knowing what he had to do, he made no move to pick the weapon up.

"Something I can do for you, Dicks?" Morton Lewis inquired, knowing the sheriff had no liking for the Christian name he had been given by his parents and feeling they were on sufficiently good terms to be able to dispense with more formal greetings.

"You've been away for a spell, I hear?" the peace officer said, his accent that of a Kansan and making the words more of a statement than a question.

"Just over a month," Mort confirmed. "Took a young luff from the Second Cavalry and his sister hunting back of Sanchez Riley's."

"Where's Pete at?"

"I sent him off to hunt him a couple of jack rabbits while I came in. You know what he's like for whupping town dawgs. Which I reckon I've got some folks hereabouts riled up enough at me without him starting to chaw up their pets."

"Are you still riding that big claybank?"

"He's standing outside at the hitching rail," Mort replied, wondering why the normally laconic peace officer was asking the questions and subjecting him to such an intense scrutiny.

"Have you had him shod lately?" Dickson asked.

"Nope."

"Then he's still got that near front shoe with the cross shaped ridge on it?"

"Yep. It doesn't fuss him none, or I'd've had it changed."

"How long have you been back?" the sheriff wanted to know.

"Just now rode in," Mort answered. "Had to pass through town, so I reckoned I'd best drop by and see what you know about ole Dexter Chass."

"I've just now come back from looking at him," Dickson said somberly. "Both him and his son are dead."

"Dead?"

"Shot in the back. It happened at least three days ago, according to Doc Benett. I found a couple of empty shells from a Spencer carbine in the bush and some real clear hoof prints, with a cross shaped ridge on the near front."

Even as the full import of the words began to impress itself upon Mort, heavy footsteps pounded along the sidewalk. The door of the office was thrown open and, led by Brenton Humboldt, several well dressed men came in hurriedly. Big, heavily built, with a thick mane of white hair, the florid state of his features and heavy breathing indicated he had come to the jailhouse in a hurry.

"I see you've got him, sheriff!" Humboldt boomed.

"I wouldn't call it 'got,'" Dickson corrected. "He just now walked in of his own accord, I didn't have to 'get' him."

"He's here, that's what counts," the banker snapped, his position of authority in the town having accustomed him to greater deference than was ever shown by the peace officer. "Arrest him for murder!"

"Murder—!" Mort began, swinging around to look at the speaker who withdrew a hurried pace before his cold stare.

"I'd want to know for sure he'd committed murder before I made an arrest," Dickson interrupted.

"Sure?" Humboldt snorted, alarm at what he believed he had read in the scrutiny from the young rancher forcing him to speak. "According to what that Mexican, Salar, was saying at the Golden Hind Saloon, you found spent cases from a Spencer carbine where the killer shot from at poor Mr. Chass and his son, and you found tracks with a distinctive horseshoe like one on his horse out there."

"Salar talks too much," the sheriff grunted, the man in question and two other hands from the Standing DMS ranch having brought news of the double killing and accompanied him to investigate.

"Are you saying he was lying?" the banker demanded.

"Just that he talks too much," Dickson corrected.

"He told me when I asked in my capacity as justice of the peace," Humboldt asserted. "And it is in that capacity I have come to see you. Was Mr. Salar telling the truth, or not?"

"That's what we found—!" the sheriff began.

"Then what more proof do you need to make the arrest?" the banker snapped and his companions, all citizens of importance and influence in their own right, muttered a sycophantic concurrence.

"I haven't been given time to ask *Mr. Lewis* any questions yet," Dickson pointed out, refusing to be daunted by the realization that the assembled group formed a powerful force in the town and could make his work difficult if they wished. He was too experienced to continue using "first name" terms when referring to the rancher under the present circumstances and his voice remained just as impersonal as he went on, "Where were you three, four days back?"

"Hunting with Lieutenant Thatcher from the Second Cavalry and his sister back of Sanchez Riley's," Mort replied, refraining from mentioning he had already given the information.

"That's Comanche country!" Humboldt put in. "Are you saying you took an Army officer and a young lady there?"

"Why not?" Mort inquired. "Jim—The lieutenant wasn't in uniform and I can go in any time with friends. Fact being, three, four days back, we were at Grandpappy Wolf Runner's village."

"Can you *prove* that?" Humboldt challenged, once again before the peace officer could speak, looking disappointed as he realized what an answer in the affirmative would mean.

"Clay Morrison knows we went there," Mort told Dickson.

"Your cook?" the banker sniffed. "He's hardly what I would call an unbiased witness."

"The lieutenant and his sister can tell you we was there." the rancher said, continuing to direct his words to the peace officer and struggling to control his rising temper.

"I'll get word to ask them," Dickson promised.

"That'll take time," Mort declared and, remembering something else, he continued, "Hey though! I can nail down one day we were there real good. Miss Thatcher did a real good drawing of her brother, Grandpappy Wolf Runner and me. She's signed it and put the date on and that was four days back."

"Let me see it!" the sheriff commanded, his tone impersonal in spite of the relief and satisfaction he was experiencing.

"I don't have it with me," Mort admitted. "She gave it to Grandpappy Wolf Runner and he's got it at the village. I can easy enough go fetch it for you."

"I daresay he would like to be given the *chance!*" Humboldt snapped, making it obvious he was speaking to the peace officer. "Well, sheriff, are you going to do your *duty* and arrest him?"

"How long would it take you to go fetch the drawing, Mr. Lewis?" Dickson asked, without so much as a glance at the townsmen.

"Three days," Mort estimated, paying just as little attention to the mutters of protest which arose from the banker and his cronies. "Two, should I ride relay on fresh hosses from the spread."

"That's out of the question!" Humboldt stated, striding forward to halt just in front of the desk. "If he goes, what guarantee do we have that he will come back?"

"You've got my word on it, sheriff!" the rancher stated, his face turning darker with suppressed rage despite the effort he was needing to exert in preventing the growing anger from becoming apparent in his voice. "The quicker I can clear myself with *you*, the better I'll be pleased. I've got a nice lil spread and I know there'll be no living there for me until I have."

"I can't *allow* it, sheriff!" the banker warned, waving an admonitory right forefinger in front of the peace officer's face. Then he indicated the men behind him with a gesture of his left hand, continuing in a pompously authoritative tone. "And I'm speaking as chairman, on behalf of my fellow County Commissioners here, as well as in my capacity as justice of the peace. You have a man here who the evidence points to as having committed two cold blooded murders—!"

"I've got what I reckon would be called 'circumstantial evidence' in a court of law where he's concerned and nothing more," Dickson corrected, also requiring to exercise restraint as he knew to do otherwise would only make the townsmen more set upon supporting Humboldt. "There's more than just *his* Spencer around, in fact I've not even had time to check what caliber shell it uses."

"And the hoof prints you found?" the banker challenged.

"They *could* match those of that horse of his outside," the sheriff admitted. "But, should he have shot the Chasses, I don't reckon a man with his knowledge of scouting and cutting sign would have ridden a horse which could be traced back to him so easily, much less cross ground that was soft enough to leave real clear prints."

"You're making a very good case for your *friend!*" Humboldt asserted.

"I'm figuring on looking at things from all sides," Dickson answered coldly. "Isn't that what I'm hired to do?"

"You're hired to uphold the law!" the banker declared, to the mumbled agreement of his companions. "And, under the circumstances, I fail to see how you can justify allowing this man to go where he will be safe from arrest should he decide not to return."

"You can send one of the boys from the spread, sheriff," Mort offered, realizing Humboldt was expressing a point of view which would be shared by many people in the town and having no desire to place the peace officer's appointment in jeopardy. "They can do it easy enough."

"But they would hardly be what I would consider unbiased witnesses," the banker commented in a judicial fashion, attempting to display complete impartiality and the impression that he was solely interested in ensuring justice was done. He refused to so much as glance at the tall young man who had aroused his animosity, "Nor, as *you* know, sheriff, would a court of law consider them to be."

"Could anybody else go and fetch it?" Dickson asked, conceding there was some justification in the point he had just heard.

"I'd give you my medicine pouch," the rancher offered. "That would get you to Grandpappy Wolf Runner, happen you carried it in plain sight and rode in the open."

"Or whoever I sent?" the sheriff inquired.

"Sure," Mort confirmed. "Any *Kweharehnuh* they come across would know they'd been sent by me and take them to Grandpappy."

"Then that's what I'll do," Dickson decided, starting to stand up. "So I'll take your gunbelt for starters."

"Why?" the rancher demanded.

"I'll have to hold you here until I've got this settled," the sheriff replied, glancing at the barred door which gave access to the cells in the rear section of the jailhouse.

A cold sensation bit through Mort on hearing and realizing what was meant by the words and involuntary gesture. Remembering the warning given by Healing Hands, even though he felt sure Dickson was not the enemy he believed to be a friend, his every instinct suggested he had walked into a carefully prepared trap. Nor, after a moment's thought, did he consider it was laid by Humboldt. While the banker apparently felt enough hatred to behave in such a fashion, the rancher doubted whether he would set about obtaining revenge in such a roundabout manner. Furthermore, he had never been on such good terms—even prior to the association with Rose Humboldt—to be regarded as a friend.

One thing the rancher concluded was certain. The enemy who had set up the clever trap was certain to have covered all contingencies, and steps would be taken to prevent him proving he had not killed the Chasses. Therefore, whoever was sent to collect the drawing would have to run the gauntlet of men under orders to stop it being brought back. Furthermore, once word got out that he had such a strong alibi, his unknown enemy was unlikely to sit back and wait for his innocence to be established. Competent as Dickson undoubtedly was and backed by two reasonably efficient deputies, there were far too many ways in which a prisoner held in the cells could be killed.

In addition to the assumptions he had drawn, there was something else compelling Mort not to want to do as the sheriff suggested. As a result of his upbringing, he had a hatred of being confined in any way. The prospect of being held in a cell for an indefinite period, even without the danger of there being attempts upon his life during the incarceration, was more than he could bear to contemplate.

With Mort, right or wrong, to think was to act!

"Stay put, sheriff!" the rancher commanded, grabbing Humboldt by the scruff of the neck with the left hand while the right brought out the Colt 1860 Army revolver, cocked its hammer and thrust the muzzle at his double chin.

"What the—?" Dickson began, but did as he was told.

"I'm going out of here—!" Mort stated.

"Don't be a fool—!" the sheriff commenced.

"I'd be worse than a fool was I to let you put me in a cell," the rancher claimed, feeling the banker trembling with what he suspected was a mixture of fear and rage. "You *know* it wasn't *me* made wolf bait of the Chasses, but I'm not going to be given the chance to prove it."

"You'll get a fair trial," Dickson promised, throwing a prohibitive glare at the men who had arrived with Humboldt and relieved at knowing that none of them were the kind to take some ill-advised action which could place his life in jeopardy.

"Only *if* I live long enough to get it," Mort replied, moving until he too could keep watch upon the banker's cronies as well as the sheriff.

"Nobody will ever lynch a prisoner I'm holding!" Dickson asserted, directing his words as much to the town dwellers as the rancher.

"I don't have lynching in mind," Mort pointed out. "But you and your deputies can't guard me twenty-four hours a day, nor cover every place I could get shot at from. No sir, sheriff, I'm not about to make it that *easy* for who-all it is's got me into this tight. I'm going to Grandpappy Wolf Runner and'll wait there until you send word by one of my boys, nobody else, that you've got Lieutenant Thatcher and his sister here to speak for me."

"I can't let you do that, Mort," Dickson warned.

"You can't do a whole heap to stop me, way things stand," the grim-faced young rancher countered.

"Come on now," the sheriff said quietly, standing like a statue and not even so much as glancing at the revolver in his gunbelt on the desk. "You know you won't use that gun!"

"You ask Mr. Humboldt here whether *he's* game to chance it," Mort suggested, pressing the Colt a little deeper into his captive's throat.

"D—Do what he says, sheriff!" the banker gasped, trying to move his head away from the cold rim of steel which was gouging into his flesh.

"Is that the way *you* want it?" Dickson inquired, determined to make sure the responsibility for the decision was established before acting.

"Y—Yes!" Humboldt confirmed, spitting out the word as if hating the taste of it in his mouth and, judging Mort by his own standards, convinced he would be killed without hesitation should there be the slightest suggestion of resistance on the part of anybody in the office. "D—Do whatever he says!"

"Back away from the desk slow and careful, sheriff," the rancher instructed, being sufficiently diplomatic to avoid reminding the rest of the men that he was formerly on good terms with the peace officer and delighted that the banker had overlooked how he would be left without any protection should he use his Colt to enforce a demand. "The rest of you, go through into the cell block and make sure you keep your hands where I can see them all the time."

"You—You aren't helping yourself this way!" Humboldt pointed out querulously, rather than in the fashion of one delivering a warning of repercussions in the future, as his companions were obeying.

"They do say the Good Lord helps them's help themselves," Mort answered and, after the last of the party had gone through the barred door, continued, "Now you, sheriff. Soon's you're inside, reach through, lock the door 'n' toss the key over this ways. Should nothing happen, I'll send Mr. Humboldt back to let you out."

"Shall I do it, Mr. Humboldt?" Dickson asked, deriving some satisfaction from the discomfiture of the banker, even though no suggestion of it showed on his face or in his voice.

"Of course!" Humboldt authorized, even before there was need for Mort to use the muzzle of the Colt as an inducement.

"So be it," the sheriff said. "Seeing's that's how *you* want it, I'll play along *your* way."

"I'm right obliged to you, Mr. Humboldt," Mort declared, watching the peace officer carrying out his instructions. "Now all you have to worry about is if whoever's trying to have me hanged for murdering the Chasses doesn't have nobody waiting outside to stop me. 'Cause, should there be, likely they won't be as careful as the sheriff about what happens to *you* when they cut in."

CHAPTER NINE

Running Proves He's Guilty

Never had time dragged by so slowly for Brenton Humboldt than it appeared to be doing as he and Morton Lewis crossed the office towards the front entrance of the jailhouse. He was all too aware that his life was in the hands of a man who had no cause to feel the slightest well being towards him. Furthermore, from all he had heard and believed, the possession of such a mixture of bloods as was the lot of his grim faced young captor created a completely cold blooded disregard for the sanctity of human life. He believed that his only hope of survival was to ensure that every wish expressed by the "half breed" was carried out immediately and to the letter.

All right now, Mr. Humboldt," Mort said, deliberately pitching his voice in a coldly menacing timbre, as they arrived at the door. "We're going out here just like we're the best of friends. *Sabe?*"

"Y—Yes!" the banker confirmed hurriedly, the employment of the Spanish word for "understand" having been accompanied by another dig from the muzzle of the Colt 1860 Army revolver against his double chin.

"Bueno!" the young rancher declared, glancing at the key which Sheriff Jerome Dickson had tossed into the center of the floor after locking the barred door to the cells. Raising his gaze to the men beyond it, he went on, "Now I know there's another way out back there. But anybody who uses it, or starts yelling afore Mr. Humboldt here comes back to turn you loose, you'll get him killed. *Sabe?*"

"Do—Do just as he tells you!" the banker demanded,

although the words came closer to sounding as if he was pleading.

"We will," the peace officer promised.

"Send word by one of my boys, sheriff," Mort instructed, returning the Colt to its holster and removing the other hand to be used for opening the front door. "'Cause I won't come back for anybody else."

"I'll do just that," Dickson promised. "I hope you're doing the right thing!"

"I roped the son-of-a-bitch, now I'll just have to ride her out," the rancher answered. *"Hasta la vista!"*

"Vaya con Dios," the sheriff responded, knowing the last words meant, "until the next time" in the Spanish spoken along the Rio Grande.

Although he had been released and the revolver was no longer held to his neck, Humboldt did not attempt to resist or escape when he was ordered to go outside. He remembered the speed with which it had been drawn to cover him and knew this had not come about by chance, but could be repeated with an equal rapidity should it become necessary. Nor, he was convinced, would the weapon merely be used to threaten if it was pulled on him again.

Recollecting what his captor had said regarding the possibility and consequences of interference on leaving the jailhouse, as he was stepping over the threshold, the banker ran the tip of his tongue across lips which had suddenly become very dry. Clearly believing something could happen, he noticed the young rancher was keeping concealed behind his bulky body, and he sensed a similar scrutiny of their surroundings was taking place to his rear.

A sigh of relief escaped from Humboldt as he saw there was nobody upon the street or its sidewalks who might possibly put his life at risk. He had realized there were men in town who could have done so. Although they usually frequented the more ancient and less luxurious Old Holbrock *Cantina,* some of the ruffians hired by David Masefield Stewart—as the rancher preferred to be known—were at the Golden Hind Saloon, including the trio who had supplied the information about the killing of Dexter Chass and his son, but fortunately none were in sight. He found their absence from view reassuring. When he had left to interview the sheriff, they had been making threats against the "half breed" they claimed must be responsible for the double murder.

"This's as far as you need come." Mort announced quietly, having taken the banker across the sidewalk and along the street to where his big claybank gelding was standing with its reins dangling over but not fastened to the hitching rail. Extracting the Spencer carbine from the saddleboot, he removed the medicine pouch and returned it. Tossing the buckskin container over the rail, he went on, "Give this to the sheriff for whoever he sends after me, and stay put right there until I've got well on my way."

Without waiting for verbal acceptance of his instructions, the rancher scooped up the reins and swung swiftly on to the saddle. Turning the horse, he set it moving at a fast trot. Despite having failed to locate anybody who might wish to prevent him from leaving, he kept a careful watch on both sides as he was riding through the town. He also listened in case Humboldt should disregard what he had said, but this did not happen and he passed beyond the last buildings without his departure being impeded in any way.

Watching the young man going away, the banker snatched out a handkerchief to wipe perspiration from his face. He was quivering with mingled fright, anger and outraged dignity. For all that, he had no intention of disobeying the orders he had received. Waiting until he considered it would be safe for him to do so, he swung on his heel and stalked rapidly back into the jailhouse.

"*Well*, Dickson!" Humboldt barked, collecting the key and, throwing the medicine pouch on to the desk in passing as he went to unlock the barred door. "What do you think of you *innocent* friend now?"

"The same as I did before," the sheriff replied, stepping into his office. "That things need more looking into and I aim to find out just what is going on."

"God damn it, man!" the banker snapped. "How much more 'finding out' do you need to do?"

"Running proves he's guilty!" one of the most syco- phantic townsmen asserted.

"That's how I see it, too!" Humboldt declared, directing an approving glance at his supporter. Then he swung a far less amiable glare at the peace officer and went on, "So what do you intend to do about Lewis?"

"Send word for Lieutenant Thatcher and his sister to come here as soon as they can—!" Dickson began, but was not allowed to continue.

"That's nowhere nearly enough!" Humboldt interrupted. "Take a posse after him straight away!"

"There's no need for that," the sheriff replied. "I know Mort Lewis better than any of you. He'll come back without needing to be fetched like he said he would."

"Not everybody has your *faith* in him!" the banker snorted. "He has to be brought back straight away."

"Like I told you, I know him," Dickson answered, won- dering whether to refer to the personal differences between Humboldt and the young rancher, but deciding this might do more harm than good. "Bringing him back won't be easy!"

"Then take enough men to make it easy!" the banker ordered. "Now listen to me, *sheriff* Dickson. I'm negoti- ating for a big investment from General Jackson Baines Hardin which will be the making of this town, but he won't make it if he hears we've so little law and order a murderer is allowed to just ride away. So either you'll take a posse after Lewis, or I want your resignation and I'll get somebody who is ready to do his sworn duty."

"That's how it goes, huh?" the peace officer asked qui- etly.

"I've my duty as I see it to the town," Humboldt claimed pompously. "And I'm sure the rest of the County Commis- sioners are behind me in doing it."

"We're with you all the way, Brenton!" the sycophant declared, hearing mutters to the same effect by the rest of the party.

"Well, *sheriff?*" Humboldt challenged.

"Seeing as you're so set on having a posse sent after Mort Lewis, I'll take it," Dickson replied. "Something tells me he might not be brought back alive if I don't."

"Are you implying—?" the banker began.

"I'm telling you how I see things," the sheriff put in, and something about him brought the indignant comments of the other townsmen to a halt. "There's one thing you had all best bear in mind. I'm nowhere near satisfied that he killed the Chasses and I'm aiming to see nothing happens to him before I've found out one way or the other what the truth is. If that doesn't suit you, then you can have my badge and I'll be riding with *your* posse as my own man whether *you* like it or not. Whichever way it goes, I aim to see Mort Lewis is brought back alive and stays that way until we've found out the rights of this business."

"Well now," Captain Dustine Edward Marsden "Dusty" Fog drawled, reining his seventeen hand uncut paint horse to a halt and gazing ahead. "What do you make of that, Lon?"

"Could be they're running a hoss race," the Ysabel Kid replied, stopping his equally large and magnificent white stallion to join his companion in studying the scene which greeted them as they topped a rim and saw several miles of rolling, bush scattered country spread ahead. Some distance away, a single fast moving rider followed by several others was approaching along the trail (formed by the wheels of numerous vehicles over the years) they were using to take them to Holbrock in response to the uncanny "medicine" message he had received. "Which being, that jasper out front on the claybank's got his-self a pretty fair head start."

"Could be we're in the middle of a 'blue norther,'" the small Texan said dryly. "'Cepting the weather's so nice and mild."

"I only said what she *could be*," the Kid pointed out. "That *hombre* way back of them's wearing a badge of some kind and's having trouble keeping his hoss moving."

"Huh huh!" Dusty grunted, accepting that his companion

had eyesight sufficiently superior to his own to be able to draw deductions when he was unable to do so. "Which means it could be a posse after a law dodger."

"Could mean," the Indian-dark Texan supported. "And, way that feller they're after's riding, I'd say he could likely out run them."

"I hear the sheriff of Holbrock County's a fair-dealing peace officer," Dusty remarked in what a stranger might have considered a disinterested fashion.

"So we're going to bill in?" the Kid guessed rather than asked, knowing the way his *amigo* thought very well.

"Might be, whatever's doing up this way, we'll need his help," Dusty pointed out. "Which it won't come amiss should we have him a itty-bitty mite beholden to us. Anyways, you've long since stopped running contraband to cheat the Government of these good old United States of their right and lawful revenue and shouldn't get all skittish every time anybody says you should help the law."

"Old habits die hard," the Kid countered, knowing it was useless to deny he had done such a thing in the past. However, the banter had served to let his companion and himself examine the situation. Becoming more serious, even though the timber of his voice changed little, he continued, "Happen we go lay for that jasper in the bushes where the trail bends so sharp, he's like to come on us afore he knows we're anywhere around."

"Was thinking that myself," the small Texan admitted, then gave a snort of what seemed like disgust. "Hell, I've been around you so long, I'm getting the same kind of sneaky mind!"

"Why sure," the Kid answered and set his horse—which contrived to look as wild and dangerous as any free ranging *manadero*,[1] despite the trappings of domestication—into motion. "They do say a man should allus learn from the *best!*"

"I said I'd picked it up from *you*," Dusty objected, as

1. Manadero: *master stallion of a herd of wild horses. J.T.E.*

his mount also started moving in response to the signal given by his heels.

"It was *me* I meant," the Kid claimed, reaching down to slide the Winchester Model of 1866 rifle from its boot on the left side of his saddle. "Wonder what that jasper's done to get them hunting him down?"

"I wouldn't even want to *guess*," Dusty stated. "But, going by the number who're after him, it could be something pretty bad."

Having made the comment, the small Texan guided the paint from the trail on the right and his companion went to the left. Keeping to concealment as much as possible, they made for the point suggested by the Kid.

Despite the banter which had passed between them, neither Texan for a moment underestimated the gravity of the situation. Nor were they allowing it to lead them into dangerous over confidence. As far as they could discern, the man on the claybank was unaware of their presence and they wanted to prevent him discovering they were in the vicinity in time to take some kind of action. At that period, they had only served as peace officers for a few weeks in Quiet Town, Montana. However, each possessed a natural sense of tactics and could appreciate the difficulties arising from achieving their purpose. As they did not know why he was being pursued, neither wanted to have to shoot the fleeing man if he could be captured without gun play. From what he had heard about Sheriff Jerome Dickson, Dusty in particular considered their intervention would be far from welcome should it result in the death of somebody who had committed a crime which did not warrant such extreme measures.

Arriving at their appointed positions, the Texans halted their horses so they could converge across the trail. Although they could not see the latest developments in the pursuit, from what they heard, they deduced they had arrived without being detected by the man being chased. He was continuing to ride at a gallop in their direction, but he certainly would have been sure to have turned aside and headed across country if he had realized they were waiting.

"Now!" Dusty snapped, when he concluded the moment for the appearance had come and, without drawing one of his Colt 1860 Army revolvers or the Winchester Model of 1866 carbine from its boot, he caused the paint to move forward.

Feeling the big claybank gelding flagging, Mort Lewis knew the burden of the flight from Holbrock was adding to the effects of the hard traveling to which it had been subjected since he received the message at Sanchez Riley's trading post saying Dexter Chass was causing trouble for his ranch hands. This was the reason he had elected to travel along the more roundabout route offered by the stage trail instead of making for the safety of the *Kweharehnuh* territory across country. Traversing such terrain hurriedly, a hoof inadvertantly finding a gopher hole could bring down his mount with a broken leg. Should that happen, he would be captured and returned to the town. Nor would Jerome Dickson allow him a second opportunity to escape. Therefore, his only hope was to keep moving as swiftly as possible and count upon the *brio escondido*—the Spanish term meaning hidden vigor, or stamina of a very high quality—of the claybank and his own skill as a rider to keep them ahead until the horses of the posse were played out.

Guiding the laboring gelding around a corner which had prevented him from seeing what lay beyond, the rancher was startled by the sight of two men emerging from the bushes. Judging from the way they came together and halted so as to block the trail, he knew they had not appeared by accident and he must take some action. Trying to crash between them was no use. Each sat a horse as large and powerful as his own. Nor did attempting to fight his way through offer a more acceptable solution. If he was successful, despite the black clad young man holding a Winchester ready for more immediate use than was offered by his holstered Colt, he would ruin whatever chance he had of coming out of his troubles a free man. The evidence which the Thatchers could present would clear him of the double murder, but he would still have to face the consequences for shooting down one or both of the cowhands— as their attire suggested they were—while fleeing to escape arrest.

Having drawn his conclusions, Mort tried to turn the claybank aside. With its reflexes impaired by being so tired, it was travelling too fast for the sudden change in direction. Feeling it starting to lose its balance and footing, he tried to help it recover. His efforts were to no avail and, as it was going down, he began to kick free his feet preparatory to quitting the saddle. He was just a fraction of a second too late. Although he escaped being trapped beneath it, the falling horse struck his left foot and ruined his equilibrium. Thrown aside, his instincts as a rider took over. While these helped him to avoid worse injury as he landed rolling, he was winded and partially dazed. Not sufficiently so, however, to be unaware of his Army Colt being dislodged from its holster. Gasping for breath, he tried to reach the butt as the claybank—relieved of his weight—contrived to recover and kept on its feet.

"Leave it be, *hombre!*" the Ysabel Kid commanded, springing from the back of the big white stallion to alight with his Winchester pointing at the rancher.

Looking around as he attained a posture something similar to that of a sprinter awaiting the signal to start a race, Mort realized the futility of disobeying. Although they had never met, he deduced from the all black clothing, magnificent horse and easy competence by which the rifle was handled with whom he was in contention.

"Grandpappy Wolf Runner and Chief Long Walker are blood brothers from way back, *Cuchilo,*" the rancher said in Comanche. "Will you let me go on account of that?"

"I'd admire to," the Kid replied, employing the slower tongue dialect of the *Pehnane* with an equal facility, "Only I'll have to know why you're being chased before I say, 'yes' on it."

Before Mort could offer his explanation, the first of the

posse came on the scene. They were three in number, riding in a loose arrowhead formation. He recognized them as prominent among the "warriors" hired by David Masefield Stewart. In the lead, Jacob "Slats" Scanlan was a big, burly man, a cousin of the Standing DMS's segundo, but a brutal hard case in his own right. To the left, tall, lean, swarthily handsome, José Salar was a Mexican dressed to the height of *charro* fashion yet showed no suggestion of the affinity many of his race had for cold steel. He was armed with a fancy nickel plated Army Colt in a fast draw holster, with a Sharps rifle in his saddleboot, but he had no knife visible upon his person. On the right, lanky and cadaverous in appearance, Homer "Bury 'em" Milton looked and dressed like a not over prosperous undertaker, but was deadly when it came to throwing a handgun. They were followed by more of Stewart's men.

"Stopped the son-of-a-bitch for us, did you?" Scanlan greeted, a vicious grin creasing his bristle-covered, scarred and unprepossessing face, as he reached for and unstrapped the rope from the horn of his saddle. "Good, the boss'll likely want to give you something for doing it. Should have killed him, though, but we'll soon enough 'tend to that."

Listening to the chilling words, Mort remembered what he had been told by Healing Hands and guessed who was behind his misfortunes.

"God damn it!" the rancher thought. "I know we've allus got on well enough, but I never figured Dave Stewart for a *friend!*"

CHAPTER TEN

He *Knows* He's Dusty Fog

"Just what do you reckon you're going to do?" Dusty Fog asked.

"Us boys's allus had the notion to see how a half breed'd look decorating a cottonwood," Jacob "Slats" Scanlan replied and grinned at the laugh elicited from the men around him by the comment. "So now'll be as good a time as any to find out."

"It isn't," the small Texan contradicted, throwing his right leg forward and over the saddlehorn to drop from the back of the big paint stallion more quickly than by dismounting in the conventional fashion.

"What did you say?" the burly hard case demanded.

"There'll be no lynching," Dusty elaborated, walking forward with what appeared to be leisurely strides.

For a moment, Scanlan stared at the disputer of his intentions. At a casual glance from ground level, Captain Dustine Edward Marsden "Dusty" Fog was a far from impressive figure. Seen from the back of a big horse, he seemed even more diminutive and insignificant. However, never one to overlook a possibility, the hard case swung his gaze to the black dressed Texan. He was standing with the barrel of a Winchester Model of 1866 rifle resting upon his off shoulder. Gripping it with the right hand closed about the wrist of the butt, three fingers were through the ring of the lever and the fourth curled across the trigger. If anything, while somewhat more impressive by his companion, he looked even younger and more innocent.

"You reckon you can stop us?" Scanlan challenged,

throwing a look at the other "warriors" from the Standing DMS ranch and, knowing they would support him if he should need assistance, dismounted.

"Do *you* reckon I can't?" Dusty countered, his voice as quiet and deceptive as the first warning murmur of a Texas "blue norther" storm.

For a moment, Scanlan did not answer. Never susceptible to atmosphere, he failed to draw any conclusions from the way he had been addressed. Instead, his gaze went to the weapons in the holsters of the smaller intruder's gunbelt, then took in the big paint stallion standing "ground hitched" by having had its split ended reins released to dangle from the bit.

"Two white handled guns, toted for a cross draw," the hard-case announced, nodding to signify understanding. "Big paint stud-hoss and all. Just who the hell do you think you are, beef-head, Dusty Fog?"

"Hombre," the Kid put in, before his companion could reply, voice hard beneath its pleasant and gentle tenor drawl. "He doesn't have to *think*. He knows he's Dusty Fog!"

"Yeah?" Scanlan scoffed, conforming to the belief of the unenlightened that a man who had attained the legendary status of the Rio Hondo gun wizard must be a vastly more impressive physical specimen. His eyes roamed over the speaker and, having taken in the magnificent white stallion standing like a statue in the background, went on, "And I reckon *you* must be the Ysabel Kid."

"Now how did you guess that?" the Indian dark Texas asked, looking and sounding as angelic as a bunch of well-raised choirboys meeting the bishop. "Or did good ole José Salar there tip you the 'yes he is'?"

Although the Mexican frowned and looked harder at the speaker, Scanlan was not impressed by what had been said. Instead, his gaze turned once more to the small Texan and his voice was dripping with sarcasm as he started speaking.

"All right, *Dusty,"* the hard case mocked and he waved his hand towards Homer "Bury 'Em" Milton. "This here's Bad Bill Longley and I'm John Wesley Hardon his—!"

At that moment, acting as if realizing something of the kind was required, the paint stallion moved enough for the members of the posse to see the brand it carried. Burned into the hip were two letters, a O and a D, the straight edge of the latter touching the side of the former. Although he was not a cowhand as such, along with the majority of his companions, Scanlan could read the brand for what it was.

OD Connected, owned by General Jackson Baines "Ole Devil" Hardin!

Not only was Dusty Fog segundo of this ranch, he was Ole Devil's favorite nephew according to all reports!

Briefly, a sense of alarm assailed Scanlan. Then he shrugged it off. Although the other might be the Ysabel Kid, such a short-grown runt could not be Dusty Fog.

"Tell you what, *Dusty*," the hard case went on, forgetting his intention to introduce other members of the posse by the names of equally famous gun fighters. "Happen you want us to ask *real* nice afore we make him stretch hemp, we'll up and say, 'pretty please' to you."

"*Hombre*," the small Texan replied, his voice still holding a gentle tone anybody who knew him well would have realized boded unpleasantness. "I could show you letters to *prove* who I am, but I don't reckon you could read them. One thing I do know, though. Happen you want to lynch this feller, come ahead—All you have to do is pass *me*."

"Now hold hard there, Dusty!" the Ysabel Kid protested. "You're getting to be a regular hawg in such doings. Leave me have some of them for myself!"

Even as he was speaking, so mildly he gave the impression butter would be unlikely to melt in his mouth, the Indian-dark Texan moved. In an instant, the Winchester left its place of rest on his shoulder and its lever was flipped through the operating cycle almost more swiftly than the human eye could follow. While he did not offer to turn its barrel into a position which menaced the members of the posse, the speed with which he had acted suggested he could certainly fire the seventeen rounds of the fully loaded rifle at the two shots per second advertised as possible by its makers. Such rapidity might not allow anything close to extreme accuracy, but would be sufficiently lethal against a closely packed bunch of riders at close quarters.

Having swung from the saddle of his horse, rope in hand, Scanlan was starting to walk forward. However, his raised right foot descended almost in the place it had left. Yet it was not the implied threat of the Winchester held by the baby-faced and black clad youngster which caused him to change his mind. In fact, he hardly noticed it under the circumstances. Instead, his gaze was fixed upon the small figure he had been addressing with such sarcasm.

Various things began to make themselves felt upon the far from agile and discerning mind of the burly hard case. There was a casual and seemingly relaxed air about the shorter of the cowhands. Instead of having adopted the so-called "gunman's crouch" which the uninitiated frequently employed in the hope of appearing menacing, he was standing erect with hands dangling loosely by his sides. Yet, somehow, his posture conveyed an impression of much greater potential threat than would have appeared possible on the surface.

Suddenly, such was the sheer strength of his personality, Dusty no longer looked small to Scanlan!

In an instant, the young Texan seemed to have taken on a size which made him tower over the burly hard case!

"Slats!" Salar said urgently, his English good though heavily accented in the Spanish fashion. "That *is* the Ysabel Kid. I recognize him now!"

"Only *now*, José?" the black dressed Texan inquired sardonically. "I knowed *you* straight off from back when."

Already having serious misgivings, the two comments were all Scanlan needed to convince him!

With the apparently baby-faced Texan confirmed as the Ysabel Kid, that *big* cowhand must also have spoken the truth with regards to his identity!

Therefore, after the stand he had taken, the only way the posse could hang Morton Lewis would be by removing Dusty Fog from their path. Nor was he alone on the issue. He was backed by a fighting man with the reputation for being as deadly and efficient as the Comanche warrior which the Ysabel Kid now resembled and who stood ready, willing and *very* able to give him effective support.

It was a daunting prospect!

On the surface, numbers appeared to favor Scanlan in his wish to carry out the instructions given by his cousin on behalf of their employer. However, of the dozen men present, only half were actually "warriors" from the Standing DMS ranch. While three of the town dwellers were sufficiently beholden to David Masefield Stewart to have been willing to lend at least moral support, the rest were uncommitted and more likely to decline any such an action as was contemplated. What was more, Scanlan had an uneasy suspicion that he personally would be the first target selected by the *big* young Texan if trouble started. Nor, he also suspected, was he or any of his companions sufficiently fast to prevent him from being shot down if gun play commenced.

Seeing the intended victim had risen while the conversation was taking place and was looking at the Colt 1860 Army Model which lay a short distance away, Scanlan could not restrain a worried gulp. If he tried to go and pick it up, one of the posse was almost certain to intervene. In which case, others would follow suit and guns were going to roar.

"Leave if there, mister!" Dusty ordered, having seen and drawn a similiar conclusion to the hard case. "And don't *anybody* else make a move until the sheriff, or whoever this is coming has told me what's going on."

"Whatever you say, Cap'n Fog," Mort assented, accepting to do otherwise would be futile and could loose him the support of his protectors.

Before anything more could be said or done, Sheriff Jerome Dickson came around the corner on his now badly limping horse. Bringing the animal to a halt and swinging from its saddle, although he normally would not have been so neglectful, he did not offer to look at the leg which was giving it trouble. Instead, he stalked past the rearmost members of the posse.

"What's going on, Scanlan?" the peace officer demanded, after having glanced at Dusty and the Kid.

"We've caught Lewis," the hard case replied sullenly.

"I can see that," Dickson claimed. "What's the rope for?"

Knowing how little his profession of salty toughness impressed the sheriff and remembering the posse had been warned there would be no attempts at summary justice if they caught the fugitive, Scanlan did not reply!

Being less acquainted with Dickson, but desirous of proving himself to be "wild, woolly, full of fleas and never curried below the knees," the youngest of the "warriors" elected to deliver the explanation!

"We was figuring on saving the county the cost of a fancy trial and hanging."

"I've told you there'll be no *lynching* while I'm running things!" the sheriff growled, turning to look at the speaker, despite being conscious of how little support he could count upon from the other members of the posse.

"Could be that won't be so all fired much longer," the young man replied with a mocking sneer directed towards the rancher. "What I hear, old Banker Homboldt ain't going to take kind to you being so careful about a feller's was figuring on raising half breed whelps with his daughter."

"Stay put, *Mr. Lewis!*" Dickson commanded, as Mort let out a growl of anger and made as if to lunge towards the man who had spoken. "Do as I say, damn it!"

"Hell, you can let that god-damned half breed come, happen he's so minded!" the youngest "warrior" offered truculently, watching the rancher—who had realized to do otherwise would be playing into the hands of his enemies— freeze into immobility. "I reckon I can stop him afore he's took two steps!"

"*Hombre, he* doesn't have a gun," the Kid put in, speaking with what sounded to be a meek and gentle voice although his demeanor indicated he was neither. Rather he gave the impression of being as ready to erupt into sudden and violent motion as a cougar crouching for a charge. "Which I reckon you've already took into account. Now me, I'm part Comanch', same as he is. So, happen you've a mind to burn that "half breed" brand on me, get to doing her and I'll come right on over to see can you stop *me* and my ole yellowboy afore we've took them said two steps."

"Keep your god-damned yapper shut, Tim!" Scanlan snarled over his shoulder, the warning being elicited by his belief that a hostile act upon the part of the loud mouthed young "warrior" would almost certainly bring part of the Texans' wrath upon him.

"Damned if he's not a whole heap smart'n he looks," the Kid declared and went on to confirm the hard case's suppositions. "See, *hombre*, he knows that come's gun play, 'less Dusty beats me to cutting loose, he'll be the *second* of you to die. And, should I open up, I aim to keep throwing lead regardless until my ole yellowboy's emptied out. Which not all of it's going to be needed for *you*."

"I couldn't have put it better myself, Lon," the small Texan praised, although he considered the point had been made adequately by his *amigo*. The man who had provoked their intervention was glancing around and finding that the other members of the posse were looking distinctly uneasy at the prospect facing them. Turning his attention to the peace officer, he continued in a more polite tone, "I'm Dusty Fog, sheriff. Do you mind if the Ysabel Kid and I ride into Holbrock with you and your prisoner?"

Dickson suspected a joke for a moment, or that a piece of attempted aggrandizement had led to the adoption of the two famous names. However, there was no suggestion of amusement or the kind of bombastic truculence which would have accompanied the second alternative. Then, being a man of discernment and with a shrewd assessment of character very useful in his present line of work, he saw beyond mere external appearances and knew the pair were who they claimed to be. He also deduced why nothing had happened to Mort Lewis prior to his arrival.

If the sheriff had needed further confirmation to support his judgement, the glance he took at the members of the posse supplied it. Like Scanlan, Salar and Milton were making sure their hands were prominently displayed well clear of the butts of their respective weapons. There was an equal eagerness to exhibit pacific intentions on the part of the other "warriors," all of whom were glowering in a threateningly prohibitive fashion at the provoker of the potential danger. The town dwellers Dickson suspected of being eager to earn the approval of David Masefield Stewart were moving their horses away from the Standing DMS hands.

"I'd be pleased to have you along, Captain Fog, Kid," the sheriff declared, then looked at the rancher. "Pick up your Colt and come hand it and your knife over, Mort. You're coming back with us."

"Whatever you say, Dicks," the rancher assented.

"Should *anybody* reckon they can make out they figured he was fixing to turn that hawg-leg on 'em," the Kid announced. "They'd better say their prayers *afore* they make their move, 'cause there won't be no time for them to do it after and they won't be going to hell *alone*."

Conscious of the hate filled eyes which wanted him, Mort collected his revolver from where it had fallen. Holding it by the barrel, he took out and grasped the knife by the center of the blade. Having done so, he walked over and presented them to the peace officer with a gesture of resignation.

"That's fine," Dickson said quietly. "As soon as I've found out what's wrong with my horse, we'll go back to Holbrock."

"It's none of my never-mind, sheriff," Dustry drawled. "But do you reckon there's need keep all these fellers waiting for us?"

"There isn't," the peace officer confirmed.

"Let's get going, boys!" Scanlan ordered, deciding the wisest course was to return to town and inform his cousin of how the situation had turned out.

"Is Mr. Stewart likely to be in today?" Dickson inquired, as the hard case was walking to his horse.

"Nope," Scanlan replied, swinging on to the saddle. "He's gone over to Austin for a spell on business, but Cousin Leftie's waiting for us at the Golden Hind."

"I'll be seeing him when I get back," the sheriff promised.

"You bunch," the Kid supplemented. "I wouldn't want you to think I don't trust you, 'cause I *don't,* so make sure I can see you all the time as we ride in."

CHAPTER ELEVEN

I Don't Do No Fist Fighting

"Looks like you've got a welcoming committee, Dicks,"
Captain Dustine Edward Marsden "Dusty" Fog commented,
studying the crowd assembled outside the jailhouse.

"Might be those high mucky-mucks're waiting to say
they're so pleasured by the way you've done your duty,
they're figuring on raising your pay," the Ysabel Kid went
on.

"That's about as likely as you voting Republican," Sheriff
Jerome Dickson claimed dryly.

"I always thought he did," the small Texan declared, then
grew serious. "Would they be Mr. Brenton Humboldt and
the rest of the County Commissioners?"

"They would," the peace officer confirmed.

"Wouldn't've been one of them's did the meaness to your
hoss, you reckon?" the Kid inquired.

"I can't say I like any one of them," Dickson replied.
"But I'd be inclined to say more 'no' than 'yes' to that.
Besides which, none of them would have had a chance to
do it between me passing the word I was taking a posse
after Mort and leaving."

On examining his horse, the peace officer had discovered
a tendon in its near front leg had been nicked—but not
fully severed—by a well placed thrust from the thin and
very sharp blade of a knife. He knew this was an old trick
practiced to adversely affect the performance of a racehorse.
Its value arose from the effects of the injury not becoming
obvious until the animal was being used and lameness de-

veloped.[1] There had been several members of the posse
waiting at the livery barn when he had arrived to collect his
horse, including some of the Standing DMS ranch hands,
who had not come along. However, of one thing the sheriff
felt certain. The only hostler on duty was a friend of long
standing and the injury could not knowingly have been
inflicted in his presence. On the other hand, a skilled op-
erator could have done so while he was distracted in some
fashion. Even without knowing the animal might be crippled
permanently. Dickson promised himself he would try to
discover who was responsible and take punitive action.

Clearly, having taken the warning given by the Kid to
heart, Jacob "Slats" Scanlan and the rest of the "warriors"
had set off while the examination of the horse was being
carried out, and they made sure they did as he had stipulated,
even though traveling at considerable speed. However, as
had been the case with the other town dwellers, the trio who
felt obligated to David Masefield Stewart had elected to
wait until the sheriff was ready to return. In fact, wishing
to avoid being suspected of collusion in the intended and
thwarted lynching of Morton Lewis, two had offered to share
a mount and allow Dickson to use the horse this made
available.

There had been little conversation during the return journey. Nor, when there was talking, had the subject been the
double murder of Mort's attempt to escape. Neither had
Dusty and the Kid referred to their reason for having been
in the vicinity. While interested in the latter, the sheriff and
the rancher knew that this apparent lack of curiosity regarding the murder and Mort's escape was not caused by
disinterest. They were willing to wait until a more propitious
time before learning in what they had become involved.

"Shall we go and doff our hats polite-like when they start
cheering you, Dicks," Dusty inquired, having discovered

---

1. *The trick was known amongst the horse racing fraternity of Great—
as it was then—Britain, see:* Case One, "Silver Blaze," THE MEM-
OIRS OF SHERLOCK HOLMES, *by Sir Arthur Conan Doyle, J.T.E.*

how the sheriff preferred to be addressed by those he considered his friends.

"Let's make them come to *us*," the peace officer replied.

Having delivered the pronouncement, Dickson turned his borrowed mount from the main street. Once his party was concealed from the group outside the jailhouse, he dismounted. Having told a couple of the town dwellers to take his injured horse and the claybank gelding belonging to the rancher to the livery barn, he sent the rest to resume their interrupted business. Asking if Dusty and the Kid wished to put up their stallions, then join him later, he was relieved to hear they were willing to leave this until after they had accompanied him to his office and learned "what was doing." Remembering something said by Humboldt, he considered the presence of the small Texan might prove advantageous in the interview he suspected would soon be taking place.

Accompanied by the two Texans, on foot and leading their horses, the peace officer escorted Mort to the rear of the jailhouse. Unlocking the back door, after a momentary unaccustomed stiffness of the mechanism, he signalled for them to precede him into the building. The barred door connecting the cell section with his office was open, although he thought he had closed it before leaving. He was not permitted time to ponder upon either matter.

Following the sheriff and peace officer across the cell portion of the building, Dusty glanced around and concluded such places rarely differed greatly in their lay-out or appearance. The office was a fair sized room, with a well used desk in the center and surrounded by a quartet of none too new chairs. Attached to one wall was a big cupboard. Facing it at the other side, a rack held several rifles and shotguns. On a board to the right of the front entrance were pinned a number of wanted posters. The whole scene, he concluded, might have been the county sheriff's office — run by his father, Hondo Fog — in Polveroso City. However, like Dickson, his attention was soon diverted from what he was doing.

For a different reason!

While the sheriff was looking to where Brenton Humboldt was unlocking the front door and entering, the small Texan was glancing out of a window. Standing on the sidewalk, Scats Scanlan pointed along the street and said something to José Salar and Homer "Bury-Em" Milton. Nodding in agreement, they followed him out of sight until shoving ahead of the crowd, they appeared in the open doorway, then came inside.

"I see you've caught him, sheriff!" the banker boomed, walking forward oblivious of who was on his heels instead of his cronies.

"I've caught him," the peace officer confirmed.

Before any more could be said, the town dwellers about to come into the office moved aside. They were sufficiently well acquainted with the temper of the big, shaggy coated, greyish dog to impede its search for its master. Tail wagging as it received a stronger scent than that which had guided it there, it entered.

"Get the hell away from me, you stinking cur!" Scanlan snarled, although there would have been more than plenty of room for the dog to pass. He stepped forward and drew back his right foot.

Despite Pete being far less dangerous than the men outside imagined, such an attitude produced a hostile response. Letting out a low growl, the dog swung towards the hard case. Even though it did not attack him, Scanlan snatched out his Colt 1860 Army Model revolver and fired. Giving a yelp of pain, as the lead seared across its head, the dog went down.

An angry shout burst from Dickson. By his side, Mort Lewis began to lunge forward without giving a thought to being unarmed. Fast though he moved, Dusty Fog acted even more swiftly. Sweeping off his low crowned, wide brimmed black hat, the small Texan lashed it into the rancher's face. Dropping it as Mort's advance was changed into a bewildered retreat due to the force of the unexpected blow, he plunged through the barred door like a living projectile.

Starting to turn his Colt so as to shoot down the rancher

in what he would claim to be self defense, Scanlan had no time to even think about the impediment to his scheme before a fist crashed against his bristle-covered jaw. Although small, Dusty was muscled like a Hercules in miniature and possessed a strength well beyond the average.[2] Furious at what had happened, and deducing why it was done, he put every ounce of power and all his weight behind his right fist. Taken by surprise, Scanlan was sent blundering helplessly against the wall by the cupboard. Although starting to fall when he arrived, he was prevented from going all the way. He was not, however, offered an opportunity to recover.

Following the burly hard case, Dusty delivered a backhand swing with his left arm. The second knuckle caught Scanlan in the center of the top lip, sending waves of agony through him. Rising after striking and reversing direction, the fist hit the side of his face and slammed his head over. Although no mean performer in a rough house brawl, Scanlan was unable to protect himself against the sheer fury of his small assailant's attack.

Giving vent to a snarled profanity, Milton darted forward with the intention of helping his companion. His hope of taking Dusty unawares came to nothing. Flying up, the small Texan's right hand jerked open one half of the cupboard's door and swung it into the lean face of the approaching hired gun. Meeting it head on, Milton's nose was smashed and spewed a spray of blood. Tottering away, half blinded by tears of pain, but with his right hand going instinctively to grasp the butt of his holstered revolver, the attempt to draw it came to nothing. Pivoting on his right leg, the small Texan sent his left foot in a kick which took and folded its recipient at the middle like a jack-knife being closed. As the foot descended, Dusty fetched up a punch with his right hand. Meeting the lowered jaw, it lifted Milton erect to send

2. *An example of Captain Dustine Edward Marsden "Dusty" Fog exhibiting his exceptional physical development and strength is given in:* MASTER OF TRIGGERNOMETRY. *J.T.E.*

him backwards and supine upon the unyielding boards of the floor.

Watching what was happening, Salar reached for his low hanging Colt. No *caballero* of pure Spanish blood, which he boasted of being, would think of descending to anything so barbarous as fist fighting. Particularly against one so clearly competent as that swift moving *big* young Texan. However, before the weapon could be lifted from its holster, he had other things than avenging the suffering of his companions upon his mind.

Thrusting the Winchester into the hands of the sheriff, who grasped it instinctively, the Kid sprang across the room. He alighted in front of the Mexican, the massive bowie knife already clear of its sheath and its razor sharp, clip pointed blade held ready to be driven in either a thrust or a belly ripping slash.

"I don't do no fist fighting neither, Salar!" warned the black dressed Texan, although at that moment his face was the cold and savage mask of the *Pehnane* Comanche Dog Soldier he could rightly claim to be. "So leave her lie, or you'll be trying to lift her with a bloody stump!"

Knowing he was not hearing an idle threat and feeling certain *Cabrito* was capable of carrying it out, the Mexican released his hold on the butt and moved the hand aside. There were limits to how far he would go for a companion and, while no coward, he considered the limits had been passed at that moment.

Granted a respite by Milton's intervention, Scanlan pushed himself from the wall. Thrusting with his hands, he gave a shove which sent the small Texan reeling to the center of the room. Then, forgetting he was still armed—despite having dropped one Colt—in his determination to repay the blows he had taken, he charged with the intention of smashing his assailant by brute strength. A low and startled exclamation burst from the sheriff at the sight. Although he had stood transfixed, amazed by the strength and sheer fury of the attack Dusty had delivered, he thought the disparity in their respective size and weight would turn the tables now the element of surprise had gone.

Before Dickson could make a move to intervene, Dusty leapt as if meaning to meet the burly hard case head on. Instead, swerving at the last moment, he caught Scanlan by the right wrist. Feeling a powerful twisting wrench given to the trapped limb, the hard case was propelled in a twirling rush towards the door. Making Humboldt leap hurriedly aside, he crashed backwards into the wall with an impact which caused some of the wanted posters to fly from the board. Given not a moment to recover, he had the small Texan's right fist sunk almost wrist deep into his belly. Starting to fold over, his shoulders were grasped and flung to smash against the wall once more. His eyes began to glaze and his body started to crumple as consciousness left him.

Filled with a cold and savage rage over the shooting of the big dog, Dusty was oblivious to the condition to which he had reduced the hard case. Catching hold of the front of Scanlan's shirt with his left hand, he pulled back the right. Instead of knotting a fist, he kept it extended with fingers together and thumb bent across the palm in the exceptionally effective way he had been taught by Tommy Okasi.

"Dusty!" the Kid yelled, knowing that some of the Japanese fighting techniques his *amigo* had learned from the man who now acted as valet to General Jackson Baines. "Ole Devil" Hardin could kill if delivered at full strength. "Leave be. The dawg's only creased!"

"And you leave that gun in leather, Leftie!" Dickson supplemented, turning the black dressed Texan's Winchester into alignment as the segundo of the Standing DMS ranch came into the office with his left hand closed about the butt of the near side Remington New Army Model of 1863 revolver. "Way I see it, that cousin of your's got what he asked for, throwing down on Pete like he did."

"There's some might not see it that way, sheriff," Wilson "Leftie" Scanlan answered, but refrained from trying to complete his draw.

"There always is," the peace officer admitted. "Let's

leave it's we agree to disagree and have them both toted the hell out of here."

"Get some of the boys to do it, José!" the segundo commanded, eyes on the cause of his cousin's bloody and battered condition as the Mexican went past to carry out his instructions. Wondering how one so small could have even survived, much less inflicted so much damage—the men from the posse having failed to find him on their return, due to his having an assignation with a married woman—he went on, "I don't know how you did it, feller, but you'd best be long gone afore he comes 'round."

"I'm aiming to be staying hereabouts for a spell," Dusty declared, having released his hold and stepping back a few paces as his victim slipped flaccidly to the floor. "So, happen you're kin with feelings for him, make sure he stays well clear of me."

"Who the hell are you?" Scanlan asked, staring harder at the small Texan and developing the impression of greater bulk which the force of his personality could create in such conditions.

"The name's 'Edward Marsden,'" Dusty partially introduced, having guessed the identity of the banker and, remembering the comment from the young hard case, wanting to learn more about the situation before supplying more detailed information.

"Sounds familiar," the segundo growled, eyes flickering to the wanted posters on the board and floor.

"Why don't you take a closer look to see if I'm on a dodger?" the small Texan suggested, making the words a challenge. "And, should I be, I'll leave it to you how you play it next."

"Running down wanted men's not *my* chore," Scanlan replied, feeling sure the newcomer did not come into such a category and deciding the moment for taking the matter of Mort Lewis further was not yet at hand. Nodding to the men who were entering led by Salar, he went on, "I'll go to the doctor's with Cousin Slats, sheriff."

"You do that," Dickson authorized. "And, after him and

Milton have had their hurts 'tended, get them out of town along with the rest of your crew."

"Mr. Stewart isn't going to take kind' to hearing you've run his boys out of town," the segundo warned.

"Mr. Stewart's away in Austin for a spell, what I hear," the peace officer answered. "And I'll be right here should he want to complain when he comes back. Only you tell him, afore he does. I don't take kind' to fellers riding in a posse I take out trying to lynch the man I'm after when they catch him."

"I'll keep it in mind," Scanlan promised.

Although little showed on his face as he was leaving the office behind his companions, the segundo was seething with rage.

Up until hearing the posse had returned with Mort Lewis alive, Scanlan had been satisfied that everything was going even better than anticipated. Following a revision of the scheme proposed by Dennis "Waxie" Corovan, a horse had had the appropriate shoe prepared to add to the "evidence" which would incriminate Mort Lewis. There had been no difficulty in murdering Dexter Chass and his son, using a Spencer carbine the segundo had borrowed from one of the "warriors." After this, the timing of the affair had been even better than he had dared to hope. Not only had the bodies remained undiscovered, due to the unsociable and inhospitable reputation of the family, but the intended victim— brought by information received at Sanchez Riley's trading post—had returned on the day the sheriff was told about the killings.

Although the rancher had gone straight to see Dickson on his arrival, his escape and flight had presented an opportunity which Scanlan had sought to exploit. Ordering his cousin and other of the "warriors" to go with the posse, he had not joined them. In addition to wanting to avoid giving too much proof of collusion, he had seen he would have a chance of dalliance with the wife of one of the town dwellers who had offered to go in the hope of gaining the approbation of his employer. Acting upon his instructions, Salar had contrived to injure the horse to be used by the sheriff. By doing so, it was hoped Dickson would be unable to keep up and prevent the young rancher from being shot while fleeing, or lynched should he fall into the hands of the pursuers.

Seeing the crowd gathered outside the jailhouse as he was leaving the unfaithful wife, Scanlan had been on his way to investigate when his cousin, Milton and Salar entered the building. Noticing the big dog going in shortly after and hearing the shot, he had guessed what was intended. However, on arriving, he found things had gone badly amiss. Instead of having provoked the intended victim into an act which would allow him to be gunned down for what would pass as self defense, perhaps even the sheriff meeting a similar fate, he had found Slats and Bury-'Em unconscious and Salar standing like a statue before the threat of the bowie knife in the hand of the second newcomer.

"Who the hell were those two beef heads, Jose?" the segundo demanded.

"Dusty Fog and the Ysabel Kid," the Mexican replied. "They stopped Lewis on the trail, but wouldn't let us do anything to him. What do we do now, *amigo?*"

"What we started out to do," Scanlan replied.

"With them backing Dickson?" Salar inquired.

"If they do, they'll get taken out along with him and Lewis," the segundo claimed, remembering something he had heard about the plans which were being formulated by Humboldt and how Ole Devil Hardin was involved. Suspecting Dusty Fog might have come to Holbrock to discuss this matter, he considered he might be able to kill two birds with one stone. "The boss'll like *that,* only doing it's going to cost him a pretty fair sized bonus for us when we're through."

CHAPTER TWELVE

This Could Be Why We're Here

"You say those men tried to *lynch* your prisoner, sheriff?" Brenton Humboldt asked, after the "warriors" from the Standing DMS ranch had left the office, refusing to refer to Morton Lewis by name in spite of realizing how such an act might have affected the hopes he had for the future of the town as well as himself.

"They did," Sheriff Jerome Dickson confirmed, passing the Winchester Model of 1866 rifle he was holding to its owner who accepted it after sheathing the massive James Black bowie knife.

"Mr. Chass and his son were well liked," lied the chief of the banker's sycophants, seeing what he believed was a chance to further ingratiate himself in that direction. He and the rest of the County Commissioners had entered the jailhouse when the departure of the "warriors" left space for them. Without allowing anybody else a chance to comment, he went on, "So, while they might have acted a trifle hastily, they were merely wanting to see that justice was done."

"I always thought a court of law had to decide that," Captain Dustine Edward Marsden "Dusty" Fog remarked, from where he was examining the wounded dog with its owner. "Fact being, way it's always been taught to me, in these United States, a man is innocent until a jury's heard what it's all about and found him guilty."

"He *is* guilty!" the sycophant declared. "There's been bad blood between him and old Dexter Chass for years."

"Had they got to throwing lead at one another afore this?" the small Texan wanted to know.

"Well, no," the sycophant admitted reluctantly, then nodded at the young rancher. "But you know what men like him are like!"

"*Half breeds,* huh?" Dusty hinted, sounding as if he was impressed by being consulted by a person of such obvious superior intellect and social status.

"Yes, although I suppose '*white Indians*' might be a more polite term," the sycophant replied smugly and as if conferring a favor upon Mort by his magnanimous correction. "You know how dangerous the Indian blood they have makes them."

"I've allus heard tell it do," the Kid drawled, cradling the rifle across the crook of his left arm and darting a glance of what the speaker took to be contempt at the rancher. "Had this *hombre*'s got made wolf bait been scalped?"

"*Scalped?*" the sycophant repeated, then he nodded in understanding and a note of disappointment came into his Mid-Western voice as he continued, "Well, *no*. Not that I know of. Why?"

"I allus thought Injuns took scalps when they'd counted coup on the white-eye brother," the black dressed Texan explained, oozing what seemed to some of his audience to be all the innocence of a new born baby. "'Course, this *hombre* being only half an Indian, likely the feller'd only have been *half* scalped."

"I don't know anything about *that!*" the sycophant asserted, his antipathy towards over familiar cowhands who were rarely respectful of his dignity returning. "But those men who wanted to ly—to take the law into their own hands, if they really did, might have been wanting to avenge a friend."

"Mister," Dusty said, straightening up as he saw Pete was beginning to regain consciousness. "They *really* meant to *lynch* this gent."

"A—As I said," the sycophant replied, his tone losing some of its truculence because he wondered how he had regarded the blond haired cowhand as being *small*. "They might have thought they were avenging a friend as the law wouldn't do it."

"Hombre," the Kid almost purred, except that he no longer looked or sounded innocent. "I don't know how much doings *you've* had with paid guns like them, but I've knowed their kind since back when. One thing I learned real early about them. They *wouldn't* even try to avenge their own mother was you to rape her, 'less you hadn't paid 'em to do it first."

"I'll go along with the Kid on that," the peace officer declared. "And now, *gentlemen,* I'd be pleased if you'd clear my office and leave me get on with my work."

"Are you telling us to *leave?*" the banker demanded, and the rest of the civic dignitaries rumbled their indignation at such a lack of respect from a public servant whose salary they helped to pay.

"Only the rest of them, Mr. Humboldt," the sheriff corrected calmly. "I'd like you to stay in your capacity as justice of the peace—Oh, by the way, I should have done so sooner. Allow me to present Captain Dusty Fog."

"Captain Dusty Fog?" the banker echoed, staring in the direction indicated by the peace officer as if unwilling to believe the evidence of his eyes and ears. *"The* Captain Dusty Fog, General Hardin's nephew?"

"The Captain Dusty Fog," Dickson confirmed, with barely discernible malicious delight as he studied the effect of the introduction. "General Hardin's nephew."

"G—Good afternoon, Captain Fog!" Humboldt greeted, offering his right hand to be shaken and feeling the strength with which it was grasped. "I trust you left the General in good health?"

"Well enough," Dusty admitted.

"Would you care to come to my office?" the banker asked. "Or perhaps you would rather we went to my house so you can rest after your journey before talking."

"Neither, just yet," the small Texan refused, with an icy politeness which was far different from the tone he had used while addressing the sycophant. "Seeing as how my hand and I got mixed up in this, I'd rather find out what's going on before I do anything else."

"Whatever you say, Captain Fog," Humboldt assented immediately, then looked at his fellow town dwellers. "I think we can leave matters in Sheriff Dickson's hands, gentlemen."

"How's Pete, Mort?" the peace officer inquired, barely able to conceal his amusement over the way in which the rest of the County Commissioners left the office without offering any protests, and considering he could return to first name terms with the rancher.

"Nicked and likely none too steady on his pins," Mort replied, watching the big dog struggle on to its feet and stand swaying. "But he's been hurt a heap worse in his time and come through. *Gracias,* Cap'n Fog."

"*Es nada, amigo,*" Dusty replied, then smiled and went on in English. "I hope your teeth didn't hurt my hat."

"I tried not to bite too hard on it," the rancher replied, also smiling, as he glanced at the object in question which was lying where it had fallen after striking and preventing him from dashing into the office to try and avenge the shooting of Pete. Realizing now that he had been intended to behave in such a manner, providing an excuse to kill him, he went on. "Shall I fetch it for you?"

"Nope," Dusty refused and looked at his black clad companion. "My man here can do it while you give your dog a drink."

"Get some water from the pump in back and use a wash basin, Mort," Dickson authorized.

"I'll 'tend to him for you," the Kid offered, guessing Dusty did not want their close association emphasized for some reason and this was for the benefit of Humboldt, as the peace officer and the rancher were already aware he was more than an ordinary hired hand.

"*Gracias, Cuchilo,*" Mort replied. "Go with him, you fool critter and, happen you bite off his leg, stop at the knee."

"Happen you bite me," the Kid warned, looking at the dog while retrieving Dusty's hat. "I'm going to sic my ole hoss on you and he's a heap bigger'n you."

"Shall we sit down and talk this out, gentlemen?" the small Texan asked.

"Yes," Dickson agreed and, being human, could not resist throwing a pointed glance at the banker. "I reckon it could do with a *thorough* airing."

At that moment, the scheme upon which Brenton Humboldt was basing his hopes for the future prosperity of Holbrock as well as his own hung in the balance. Basically a fair minded man, he realized that he had been allowing his personal feelings towards the young rancher to cloud his judgement. Recollecting remarks which had been made to the sycophantic Commissioner, he suspected the *big* Texan representing General Jackson Baines "Ole Devil" Hardin had at least some idea of his behavior earlier. To be fair to him, however, he felt he should do something to make amends even without such an inducement.

"I think, Sheriff Dickson," the banker said quietly. "In view of what has passed between Mr. Lewis and myself, I have no right to act in the capacity you require and will leave."

"I'd sooner you stayed, sir," Mort declared, before the peace officer could speak. "Fact being, I'd be right obliged if you would."

"Very well, sir," Humboldt accepted, for once feeling humbled. "And I thank you for asking me."

"Hell's fires, Dusty!" the Kid ejaculated, some minutes later, after Dickson had told them of the discoveries at the Chass ranch. "This could be why we're here."

"How do you mean?" the banker asked.

"Take it's *somebody*, like whoever hires those yahoos' who started yelling hang-rope, wanted to get both ranches," the black dressed Texan suggested. "He's got at least one jasper, Salar, who's got the know-how to rig the sign so's it'd point to Mort here having done the killings."

"That's a possibility," Humboldt admitted. "But, if it is the case, Mr. Lewis would be able to establish his innocence."

"So long as he stayed alive to give the sheriff time to do

it," the Kid added. "Which those *hombres* weren't figuring on letting happen."

"Jumping you and running out gave them the chance to do it," Mort admitted.

"We hadn't been giving you much of a reason to expect a fair hearing," replied the banker, to whom the comment was directed. "But I still don't understand what your man meant, Captain Fog. Surely you've come to see me about the proposition I made to the General."

"I was coming *after* we'd delivered a herd to Fort Sumner," Dusty replied. "But Lon was let know we'd be needed hereabouts before that was done."

"Let know?" Dickson queried, looking at the black dressed Texan.

"I can't tell you how, 'cause I don't know nothing about it myself, 'cepting it *works*," the Kid answered, lounging back on the chair he had been given and completely at his ease. "But I was let know that something was doing down this way and we was needed here."

"And I figured it was important enough to send the herd on and head right over," Dusty supplemented. "Which, happen you're right, Lon, I was right."

"You're way out beyond my sight, Dusty," Dickson declared, having come to first name terms with the small Texan on the ride to Holbrock, and the banker showed a similar lack of comprehension without speaking.

"Mort's grandson of Chief Wolf Runner," the Kid supplied, receiving a nod from his *amigo*. "Which, should he have got killed and that way in particular, your town'd've been hip deep and crawling with *Kweharehnuh* Comanch' bucks looking for evens."

"But how could they have known about it?" Humboldt inquired, showing none of the scepticism which would have greeted the information at another time.

"The same way their medicine man knowed somebody was out to do meaness to Mort," the black dressed Texan replied. "And got word to me, hoping Dusty and me could get here to stop it."

"You can believe Lon that such things are possible, Mr. Humboldt," the small Texan declared. "At least, I've got enough faith in him to have come straight away."

"Will they still come?" the banker asked worriedly, satisfied he was hearing the truth.

"That depends," the Kid drawled, once again having received a signal from Dusty to do the talking. "Should they figure Mort's still not out of the deep and piney woods, they'll be up and riding."

"You could go and tell them you're safe, Mr. Lewis," Humboldt suggested. "And stay with them until we have heard from that young Army officer."

"There's some real smart brains behind this game, 'though they're short on Injun savvy," the Kid warned, before either the rancher or the sheriff could speak. "Happen we let Mort go, or figuring we might, they'll likely have this town so careful watched he'd be hard pushed to get through. Or, should he, they'd follow and, was they to kill him on the way, the pot'd come to a boil quicker'n a weasel-chased jack rabbit heading for home."

"Then we could send somebody else," the banker suggested. "One of your deputies, sheriff."

"They're both out and about 'round the county," Dickson replied, opening the left side drawer of his desk. "But Rube from the livery barn would go and with your medi—Hell's fires. It's gone!"

"What has?" Dusty asked, surprised by the vehemence of the reaction from the normally composed and impassive peace officer.

"Mort's medicine pouch was in here!" the sheriff explained, indicating the drawer. "But it's not there any more!"

"But you locked up before you left," Humboldt reminded, thinking uncomfortably about the key he had in his possession.

"How many keys are there?" Dusty asked, remembering the front and rear entrances of the jailhouse had been locked on their arrival.

"My two deputies have one each," Dickson answered, but was not allowed to go on.

"I have one for the front door," the banker admitted, reaching into his trousers' right side pocket.

"Whoever took the medicine pouch didn't come through the front door," the sheriff claimed. "I thought the lock at the back was stiff when I turned it. So, especially as the door to the cells was open when I know I'd left it shut, I'm guessing the lock was picked. You called it right, Kid. There are some mighty smart brains behind this business."

"So it seems!" Humboldt breathed. Then, sucking in a deep breath, he went on, "Is there any other way you can have a message sent to Wolf Runner, Mr. Lewis?"

"Sure there is," the Kid declared, as the rancher was about to reply. "I'll take it to him."

"Will it be *safe* for him to go?" the banker inquired and he was not guided merely by the desire to give an impression of being concerned over the welfare of somebody he had begun to suspect was closer to Captain Fog than he and the other County Commissioners had been led to assume.

"Safe or not, she's got to be done," the Kid asserted soberly. "Which, took all 'round, I reckon I'm the best one to have a stab at doing it."

CHAPTER THIRTEEN

My Lodge Oath Is To Kill Him

Letting out a sharp snort and making a tossing movement with its shapely head, the magnificent white stallion—its body patched with a black powder, a product developed during days of border smuggling, to make it look like a "skewbald"[1]—caused the Ysabel Kid to wake from the nap he had been taking on the lightweight, almost skeletal, Comanche warrior's saddle he had borrowed from the hostler at the livery barn in Holbrock.

Training as a boy, which had been improved by having spent the majority of his eventful young life in situations of a precarious nature, had conditioned the Kid to come from deep sleep to total wakefulness without even a brief interim period of dull witted somnolence. The moment his eyes opened, he set about discovering what had disturbed the stallion. A glance informed him that his mount was looking towards a clump of flowering dogwood bushes about fifty yards to his right.

Instantly, knowing whatever danger might be threatening would originate from the direction indicated by the stallion, the Kid slipped sideways to the left of the saddle. By doing so, he was partially concealed behind Blackie. Even as his feet touched the ground, he was slipping the Winchester Model of 1866 rifle—which he had been carrying across the crook of his left arm, despite having been dozing—out of the *Pehnane* medicine pouch which was covering it.

1. A "skewbald" horse is colored by irregular patches of black and white and a "paint" is white with any other color. J.T.E.

"You did that real well, *Cuchilo*," called a feminine voice, speaking Comanche in the fashion of the *Pahuraix* band, and with a somewhat mocking timbre. "But only a Quick Stinger would fall asleep while riding in the daytime."

"Come out, sister," the Kid replied, with the accent of a *Pehnane*, returning the rifle to its extemporized boot and stepping from behind the stallion. "I knew there was no danger. My horse told me you were only a *naivi* of the *Par-Kee-Na-Um*."[2]

Even as the young Texan was speaking and watching the bushes being stirred by something other than the gentle breeze which had carried the warning scent to the big stallion, he was puzzled. From the sound of the voice, he had felt sure he was being addressed by a female Comanche who was still young enough to be classed as a *naivi*, maiden, rather than a *hervi*, mature woman. Yet her words were far less deferential than he would have expected to be uttered by a person of that category to a name-warrior of his standing.

No matter how much they might differ in some aspects of their respective ways of life, the Kid knew the various bands of the *Nemenuh* had one thing in common. Despite the prominence attained by a few medicine women, they all lived in a society where men were dominant. In the scales of value established by the braves, a woman was regarded as being more useful than a food dog, yet less worthwhile than a pack mule and far below a good saddle horse or a repeating rifle.

Having been raised in accordance with such standards, or so the fluency with which she employed the Comanche language suggested, the speaker should have been far more respectful in her greeting. However, over the years, the Kid had become acquainted with several young women capable of holding their own in what was still—even amongst white

2. "*Pahuraix*" *and* "*Par-Kee-Na-UM*" *are two names for the* "*Water Horse*" *band of the Comanche nation, which earned the title because its members always preferred to set up camp close to water. J.T.E.*

people—practically a "man's world." Between them, Betty Hardin, Belle "the Rebel Spy" Boyd, Martha "Calamity Jane" Canary and the lady outlaw, Belle Starr, had caused him to revise his earlier notions of masculine supremacy.[3] What was more, although he had never met one, he knew there were exceptions to the rule amongst the *Nemenuh*. Therefore, he was more interested than annoyed as he waited for his first sight of the speaker.

Not more than five foot four inches in height, the girl who stepped from the bushes looked to be in her late teens. She had the coppery-bronze skin and, although the *Pahuraix* generally tended to be slender and taller than others of their nation, the buxom build of a more typical Comanche. However, her hair and features gave indications that she had a proportion of white blood. Instead of being black, cropped to shoulder length and parted down the middle as was usual for one of her age and sex, the former was reddish brown and formed into two braids after the fashion of a warrior. While pretty, her face was broad and its brown eyes somewhat slanted, but the nose was snub rather than aquiline, making the whole more Caucasian than Indian in its lines.

The girl wore an open necked, loose fitting, multi-colored cotton shirt hanging outside faded Levi's trousers and had moccasins on her feet. In further defiance to Comanche feminine fashion, buckled around her waist over the shirt, a belt inscribed with medicine symbols carried a walnut handled Colt 1860 Army revolver with its barrel shortened by about half in an open topped high cavalry twist draw holster at the right side, and a J. Russell & Company "Green River" hunting knife was in a sheath made from wapiti hide at the left. She moved with a light footed agility which implied she was very fit and had no flabby fat on her cur-

---

3. With the exception of Belle Starr, some information respecting to all the ladies mentioned can be found in APPENDICES ONE and TWO. The lady outlaw makes "guest" appearances in several volumes of the Floating Outfit and Waco series. She and the Ysabel Kid are major participants in: Part One, "The Poison And the Cure" WANTED, BELLE STARR and THE QUEST FOR BOWIE'S BLADE. J.T.E.

vaceously firm fleshed body. A Winchester Model of 1866 carbine, its woodwork decorated with patterns made from brass tacks, dangled by its foregrip in her left hand.

"Greetings, *Cuchilo*, may you always ride well," the girl said formally, her manner that of a name-warrior addressing a social equal rather than a member of the inferior sex speaking to one of the superior gender. "We've never met, although I saw you ride *pukutsi* at the Fort Sorrel treaty meeting.[4] My name is Annie Singing Bear, but my lodge brothers call me, 'Is-A-Man.'"

"Greetings, Is-A-Man, may you always ride well," the Kid responded just as conventionally. His memory having been jogged by the introduction, he realized why the girl was behaving in a manner so untypical for one of her sex and continued, "Your name is known to me, but you are far from the *tipis* of your people."

Although Annie Singing Bear was of mixed parentage, she had spent all her life amongst the *Pahuraix* Comanche. Unlike the Kid and Morton Lewis, before the peace treaty was signed at Fort Sorrel, she had had little contact with white people. Now, having accompanied the band to the reservation to which they had been assigned, she was putting to good use the English learned from her mother by acting as interpreter between her people and the officials at the Indian Agency.

However, as a child, the girl had exhibited a proclivity towards masculine rather than feminine activities. Such a deviation from normal behavior was considered to have been ordained by *Ka-Dih*, the Great Spirit of the *Nemenuh*. Therefore, it had been accepted that she was expected to adopt the life-style—if not in a sexual sense—of a male. Accordingly, she had received the same education as would

---

4. When a Pehnane Comanche warrior "rode pukutsi," he stripped to his breech clout, made the sign of a red hand on his chest and the shoulder of his horse, then charged into the attack regardless of the odds he was facing. He was expected to emerge victorious, or die in the attempt. Why the Ysabel Kid elected to ride pukutsi is explained in: CO-MANCHE and SIDEWINDER. J.T.E.

any *tuinep'*, boy up to adolescence. Judging from the stories the Kid had heard, she had acquired all the skills required to pass from being a *tuivitsi* to the honored state of *tehnap*. Respecting the beliefs of his maternal people, he had not hesitated before employing the "man-name" she claimed to have been granted. He was certain her upbringing would not allow her to lie about such an important matter.

"I have good reason, *Cuchilo*," Annie asserted and, noticing the Kid was looking in the direction from which he had come, went on in English, "Is it safe for us to be talking out here?"

"I'm likely still being followed," the black clad Texan admitted, also reverting to his paternal language, as he started to walk forward with the stallion following on his heels like a well trained dog despite the reins of its hackamore dangling over its neck.[5] "And, give him his due, 'spite of all I've done to slow 'em down, that son-of-a-bitch José Salar can sure read sign."

Having obtained the fortuitous loan of a type of saddle which would help reduce the strain on Blackie, the Kid had made other preparations for traveling light after escaping from Holbrock. Retaining only the armament he was carrying upon his person, without even a reserve of ammunition for his rifle and Colt Dragoon revolver, he had adopted a disguise as well as changing the appearance of the stallion. Arranging for word of his "intentions" to reach and be passed on, via the man who was being cuckolded by Wilson "Leftie" Scanlan, and dressed like an ordinary cowhand instead of in his all black attire, he had set out ostensibly to collect reinforcements from the crew of the OD Connected ranch's trail herd.

Leaving the town by a circuitous route shortly after sun-

---

5. *The type of "hackamore" used by the Ysabel Kid resembled an ordinary leather halter. However, it had a headpiece something like a bridle, a browband about three inches wide which could be drawn down to cover the horse's eyes, a bosal—a rawhide loop immediately above the mouth, from the Spanish word,* bozal, *meaning "muzzle"—in place of a bit and having one-piece reins instead of a lead rope. J.T.E.*

down, the Kid had found the supposition that the track was being kept under observation was correct. Unfortunately, so efficient was the cordon arranged by the segundo of the Standing DMS ranch, he had been unable to pass through undetected and was compelled to spread warning of his departure by shooting a "warrior" firing at him from too great a distance to be disposed of silently.

Pushing on for a while, the Kid had not been made over confident by there being no immediate pursuit. Nevertheless, despite being aware of Salar's ability at "reading sign," he had stopped to rest his mount for a few hours during the night. Moving on at dawn, he had used all his considerable skill at concealing traces of his passing as much as possible despite being aware that to do so completely in the time available would be impossible with such an expert on his trail.[6] Although his tactics had delayed his pursuers, as he had anticipated, he had seen them following at a distance during one of his examinations of what lay to his rear. What was more, he believed they might have guessed where he was going prior to making for the *Kweharehnuh* village.

"Are you sure you're not just going to Sanchez Riley's to see his daughter, Rosita?" Annie challenged, after she had been told of the events leading up to her meeting with *Cuchilo*. She had reverted to Comanche as she found it easier to use than English. While listening, she had led him to where her two horse relay—each animal equipped in a smiliar fashion to Blackie and one having a bow and quiver of arrows hanging from its saddlehorn—were standing ground hitched by their dangling reins. "I've always heard you *Pehnane* do things like that."

"So do the *Park-Kee-Na-Um*, I'd reckon," the Kid countered in the same tongue. As was usual when with others of their kind they respected, the supposedly stoic and hu-

6. *Details of the methods employed by the Ysabel Kid to hide his tracks and of other incidents to which we will only be referring later in this narrative are so similar to those described in,* Part One, "The Half Breed" THE HALF BREED, *that to repeat them verbatim would merely be repetitious. J.T.E.*

morless Comanche warriors frequently indulged in a banter similar to that of cowhands under the same circumstances. "Else how'd there get to be any little *Pahuraix?*"

"Trust a Wasp to think of something like that," the girl sniffed, employing another of the names given to the *Pehnane* band. Then she became serious and went on, "Why go there instead of straight to Wolf Runner?"

"Magic Hands told me to see who left the message for Proud-Son-Of-Two-People," the Texan replied, using the name given to Captain Dustine Edward Marsden "Dusty" Fog at the time he was preventing a group of pro-Union fanatics starting an Indian uprising in Texas during the War Between The States.[7] And anything else Sanchez can tell me about what's doing in the *Kweharehnuh* country."

"They could catch up with you there," the girl warned.

"Likely," the Kid admitted. "But, happen they do, that's all their misfortune and none of my own. There aren't but six of them all told, like I said."

"Is Dead Face one of the six?"

"Dead Face?"

"Perhaps you don't know him by that name?"

"I know the son-of-a-bitch," the Kid growled, having heard of the incident during the hunt involving Dennis "Waxie" Corovan, changing to English as being more profanely expressive than Comanche. "Why'd you think *he'd* be with them?"

"According to Talks-To-Birds, he's around this neck of the woods," the girl replied, referring to the leading medicine man of the Water Horse band and resuming her maternal language. "That's why I came down this way. He led some fool *tuivitsi* on a war trail about six moons gone. None came back and one was my favorite brother by another mother. So my lodge oath is to kill them."

"He's not with them," the Texan claimed. "They all ride white, or Mex' in Salar's case. But, hell, he can't be tied in with Stewart's bunch, he'd *know* what'll happen should

7. *Told in:* THE DEVIL GUN. *J.T.E.*

Wolf Runner's brave-hearts take the war trail."

"Do you reckon that'd stop the *Namae'enuh* bastard setting it up if he figured there was money to be made from getting a full scale war going?" Annie demanded, having acquired a selection of white obscenities since living on the reservation, even though she only employed them in moments of extreme stress. "Because you don't know the "mother-something" if you do."[8]

"I know him well enough to reckon you could be right," the Kid answered. "There was enough Injun savvy in what was done for him to have sold the notion to Stewart, figuring he wouldn't know enough to guess what would happen when Wolf Runner came looking for evens. Which being, he'll be wanting to stay a long piece clear of *Kweharehnuh* country."

"Then I'll likely have to go look for him some place else," the girl said in mingled disappointment and annoyance. "Because, if I don't nail his hide to the wall, some of my lodge brothers'll be looking to do it and that'll make bad trouble for all the band."

"Could even spark off what Dusty and me're trying to stop hereabouts," the Texas supplemented. "I'm not just saying this to keep you around, mind, but maybe he's still close to Holbrock. Happen he's got as much sense as the way things've been figured out without Waxie taking cards, Stewart won't have paid him until things're settled, or close to. Might even be making him do a heap more than just talk to earn his pay, comes to that."

"I'll drift over that way and see what's doing," Annie promised. "Do you want me to see can I make trouble for those *hombres* on your trail?"

"Not that I reckon you *couldn't*," the Kid replied. "But I'd sooner you left 'em to me. Should you get shot up, your lodge brothers'll be after Dead Face themselves and we can do without *that* happening."

"Like you say," the girl assented, seeing the wisdom of

8. *See the second paragraph of our* Author's note. *J.T.E.*

what she had been told. "But I still reckon it's just, being a *Pehnane*, you're not wanting to share the coups to be counted with anybody else."

CHAPTER FOURTEEN

Kill The Half Breed

Standing in the shadows of an alley which offered a clear view into the office of the Holbrock jailhouse, some one hundred yards away, Dennis "Waxie" Corovan was filled with grave misgivings. At that moment, he hated the sight of the Remington contract-built U.S. Model of 1862 rifle — converted by the improved Ryder action, Patent Number 40,887, of December the 8th, 1863, to fire metallic cartridges — he was holding, and hated the thought of the task he had been instructed to perform. He was a sufficiently good shot to make the required hit at such a distance with the accurate weapon, but was far from enamored of the prospect of having been compelled to make the attempt. Not that his conscience was protesting over having been told to kill another human being in cold blood. Nor was he solely concerned by the remembrance that the Remington had only a single shot mechanism.

Throughout all his career as a renegade, which he had adopted voluntarily as offering a good living without the burdensome necessity of doing any hard work, "Dead Face" had always tried to avoid taking any greater risks than were absolutely necessary. The fatal war trails upon which he had persuaded inexperienced would-be warriors of the *Paruhaix* Comanche and Waco Indians to engage were not the first such affairs he had manipulated. On two other occasions, having talked equally gullible youngsters from other tribes to go on similarly disastrous raids, he had fled and left them to suffer the consequences when encountering danger. What was more, double dealing, treachery, betrayal and robbery

127

in which violence rather than guile was used, had become second nature to him. There was, in fact, no crime he was not willing to commit as long as he had seen a way to carry it out in safety.

However, Corovan had not been able to follow up all the plans he had had in mind on coming to Holbrock County and visiting the Standing DMS ranch house!

Although he had been satisfied that he had tricked David Masefield Stewart and Wilson "Leftie" Scanlan into doing as he wished, which to a certain extent he had, the renegade was not permitted to withdraw to a safe location to await developments as he had intended. Before he could do so, he had been placed under what amounted to an armed guard by the segundo and told he must take an active part in removing the owners of the two properties coveted by the rancher. He had been threatened with the most dire reprisals if he should try to escape, or to have a bounty of such size put on his head it would cause him to be hunted down remorselessly if he was successful in getting away.

On hearing that the revised plot to kill Morton Lewis had gone amiss, particularly when he was told who was responsible for the affair having come to nothing, Corovan had hoped it would at least be postponed until after Dusty Fog and the Ysabel Kid had concluded the business which brought them to Holbrock and returned to Rio Hondo County. He had quickly learned this was not to be. Despite Stewart having left to establish an alibi by visiting the State capital, Leftie Scanlan had stated a determination to do as was ordered. It had, in fact, become apparent that he was meaning to have killed the two young Texans as well as Mort Lewis and Sheriff Jerome Dickson. However, he had not offered any explanation for being willing to incur the wrath and revenge of the very efficient fighting crew of the OD Connected ranch, particularly that of the other members of it already close to legendary floating outfit.

Much to the relief of the renegade, despite the escape of the Kid at the cost of one "warrior's" life, Scanlan had not taken any hostile action for two days. Instead, he had restricted himself to merely arranging for a watch to be kept upon the front and rear of the jailhouse, and spreading a warning that any intervention upon the part of the citizens would have severe repercussions at a later date. There had been two reasons for his tactics. He wanted to learn what routine, if any, was being followed by his intended victims which might help him achieve his purpose. Also, suggesting something was being contemplated even prior to the arrival of Corovan, enough hired guns had put in their appearance at the DMS ranch house to almost double his already formidable fighting strength.

On the third afternoon, the situation had taken a change very much for the worse as far as the renegade was concerned.

Returning to the ranch house, José Salar had told Scanlan that the Kid had survived an attack upon him made at Sanchez Riley's trading post at the expense of losing the young "warrior" who had been ordered to keep quiet during the abortive attempt to lynch Mort Lewis. He had then gone into the *Kweharehnuh* country, where the pursuers had not dared to follow. Still unaware of the real reason, but knowing of the drawing which could establish the whereabouts of the rancher on the day of the double murder, the segundo had assumed he was going to collect it.

Giving instructions to the Mexican and supplying extra men to help carry them out, Scanlan had next made a statement which filled Corovan with alarm. Based upon what had been learned by the watchers of the jailhouse, the renegade was ordered to go into Holbrock after sundown and shoot Mort Lewis. By doing so, it was hoped to bring Dusty Fog and the sheriff from the shelter of the jailhouse and into the open where they too could be killed by more of the "warriors" who would charge from the outskirts.

The hopes formed by Corovan to run away and take his chances against bounty hunters later set on his trail had come to nothing!

Having known a large body of men were unlikely to move close enough without being detected, the segundo had

declared it should be possible for no more than three to do
so. Brushing aside the suggestion from the renegade that
the task would be safer if carried out alone, Scanlan had
stated his cousin and Homer "Bury"Em" Milton—who had
recovered sufficiently from the beating at the hands of the
small Texan—would act as escorts.

Given no chance of escaping, Corovan had left his horse
not too far away with those of the two "warriors" and moved
in on foot to carry out the assignment!

It had been established by the observation of the jailhouse
that Mort Lewis was being held in what was already becoming known as "protective custody." In the evening, he
was allowed to sit in the office with Dickson—whose deputies had not returned—and Dusty Fog while having supper
and until retiring for the night. By arriving not long after
the sun had gone down, it was hoped the trio would catch
their victims when they were not expecting trouble, and that
they would be given the opportunity to shoot Mort Lewis
through the windows of the well lit office.

"There he is!" Jacob "Slatts" Scanlan hissed, as Mort
came from the cell block at the rear to join the sheriff and
the small Texan at the desk. "Kill the half breed son-of-a-
bitch!"

"I'm going to cut that short growed Rio Hondo bastard
in half as he comes out!" Milton promised viciously, making
a gesture with the sawed-off shotgun he was holding.

"Like hell!" the burly hard case contradicted, making a
similar motion with the Spencer carbine in his hands which
had been used to kill Dexter Chass and his son. "That son-
of-a-bitch is *mine!*" Giving the lanky "warrior" no time to
object, he went on savagely, "Get it done, you god-damned
half breed!"

Darting a scowl of hatred at the speaker while raising
the Remington, Corovan braced its barrel against the corner
of the left side building. He was all too aware that he had
only one shot in the weapon with which to carry out his
task. Should he miss, he would not be granted another such
opportunity, as the men in the office would all take cover

before he could reload. With that in mind, he was determined to make certain of his aim. Waiting until the intended victim was sitting at the desk, he took a few more seconds to satisfy himself with the alignment of the sights. When he was ready, his right forefinger started to tighten upon the trigger.

"Get a god-da—!" Scanlan commenced impatiently, disregarding the fact that speaking at that moment could cause further delay.

Before he could finish speaking, or the rifle fired, there was a hissing sound from behind the men followed by a thud closer at hand!

The words came to an abrupt end in a croaking gasp as the hard case arched his spine in what was clearly sudden and severe agony. Allowing the Spencer to fall unheeded from his grasp, he stumbled a couple of steps forward and collapsed face down. Barely discernible against the darkness of his clothing and in the poor light, something slender rose a couple of inches from the left side of his back.

"What the he—?" Milton began, starting to swing around.

Another hiss sounded!

Once again, words were changed into a muffled cry of agony as there was a similar "thunk!"

Releasing the shotgun he was starting to raise into a position of greater readiness, the lanky "warrior's hands rose involuntarily. They clutched at the feather topped end of what felt like a straight piece of stick, although he knew it to be something far more lethal, which he was aware had impaled him so thoroughly its head had emerged through his back. Spinning around, he joined his dying companion on the ground.

Even as Corovan heard Scanlan struck, without needing to look around—although he could not prevent himself from doing so—he knew what had happened. Seeing Milton receive another arrow sent with a similar unerring aim from the darkness beyond the alley, he wasted no time in trying to locate the archer. Suspecting it was the Ysabel Kid, who had evaded the men sent to stop him returning, the renegade was aware of what to expect at his hands for having been caught trying to kill a man he regarded as a friend.

The response would be as swift and lethal as could be devised by the *Pehnane* Dog Soldier which *Cuchilo*, the Knife, could claim to be!

Throwing aside the rifle, regardless of it being his own property, the renegade fled from the alley without so much as a glance at either of his escorts. He cared nothing for their fate, being solely concerned with his own survival. Such was his state of near panic that, not until he was at some distance from the bodies did he realize he was going *away* from the horses they had left to facilitate their escape after he had fired at Mort Lewis.

Swerving to a halt behind an unoccupied building, his flight having taken him into the residential section of the town, Corovan slid the Colt 1860 Army revolver from the silk sash he used instead of a conventional holster. Peering cautiously around, he searched the area he had just traversed for the first warning sign of the Kid. Not that, he told himself worriedly, he was likely to be offered a clear view or anything better than a fleeting glimpse. Fortunately, regardless of the all black clothing generally worn by *Cuchilo*, there was a patch of open ground between them across which not even he could pass quickly if he wanted to remain unseen.

Thirty seconds crawled by!

Then a minute!

There was no disturbance!

Only the normal night time noises of a town unaware that danger was in the air!

A minute and a half passed into oblivion at a snail's pace!

Having seen nothing to alarm him through the period of *very* carefuly scrutiny, which seemed to have extended for a greatly longer time than was actually the case, the renegade gave a sigh of relief as it appeared that he might not be hunted by the killer of his companions. Now his original panic had eased, if not completely departed, he began to give more thought to what had taken place rather than devoting his attention solely to saving his life by flight.

Why had such primitive weapons as the bow and arrows been used on Slats Scanlan and Bury-'Em Milton when the Kid had, as was proved by the way in which the "warrior" who had tried to stop him leaving Holbrock had been killed, the Winchester rifle he could handle with such deadly accuracy and speed?

Obviously, having seen and guessed why so many of the Standing DMS ranch's hired guns were lurking on the outskirts of the town, *Cuchilo* had had no wish to warn them things were not going as expected!

In which case, employing the more silent means of killing would lessen the chances of the alarm being raised!

Still there was no sign of movement!

For all the evidence to the contrary, Corovan might be the only living being in the immediate vicinity!

Wondering if the Kid might have gone to the jailhouse to warn its occupants of the situation, instead of pursuing him, the renegade thought of firing shots into the air thereby causing the attack by the waiting "warriors" to be launched!

The idea was dismissed almost as quickly as it had come!

There was a chance, Corovan told himself, that he had only temporarily eluded the Kid who was now searching for him!

Or, being an acknowledged master of stalking in the darkness, *Cuchilo* might want to establish the exact position of his intended prey before starting to move across the potentially dangerous open ground!

In either case, the renegade told himself, the diversion he hoped to cause would take place too late to serve his purpose. Not only would he have betrayed his location, but the charge of the hired guns would still be too far away to prevent the Kid from reaching him before they arrived. What was more, even if his first assumption should have been correct and he was not being followed, he might meet and be shot down by some of the "warriors" who would have converged to deal with the occupants of the jailhouse.

Being disinclined to chance either of these very risky eventualties, Corovan did not cock and discharge his Colt.

Instead, he turned and moved through the blackness thrown by the shadow of the building. As he went, he was grateful for his decision which had made him don moccasins and clothing more suitable for what he was doing than the attire of a professional gambler, which he usually wore when in a town to reduce the possibility of his mixed blood being suspected. The footwear, plain dark grey shirt and brown trousers he had on permitted him to walk silently and merge into the surrounding darkness far more effectively than would have his more fancy, if never kept any cleaner, "go to town" clothes.

Alert for the slightest sound warning that the Kid might be closing in upon him, or any other indication, the renegade had some difficulty in finding his way back to where the horses were waiting. Such had been the haste of his flight, added to his being a comparative stranger to the town, that he had need to think hard and select a route after he had got what he hoped was his bearings. However, at last he found himself passing the alley from which he had been ordered to kill Mort Lewis. Glancing along it, although he could not see Milton, he was just able to make out the bulky and unmoving mound which was the lifeless body of Slats Scanlan.

Despite the lights still glowing through the windows, Corovan was unable to see into the sheriff's office from his present position. However, while he realized he could satisfy his curiosity with regards to the activities of the Kid if he could look into the sheriff's room, he did not attempt to return to the position from which he had been offered a clear view of the interior.

"Half breed am I, you stinking son-of-a-bitch!" the renegade hissed viciously at the corpse, having a deep hatred of his mixed blood despite being willing to exploit it when doing so would prove advantageous. "I wish you'd got that arrow through your god-damned guts!"

Having delivered the comment *sotto voce,* albeit with great feeling, Corovan turned to make his way to where the three horses were standing tied to the hitching rail of an animal foodstuffs store which was closed and unoccupied for the night like the majority of premises in the vicinity. He decided to take all of them with him. Not only would they allow him to travel faster in his flight from an area which had suddenly become most dangerous for him, but he derived a malicious satisfaction from the thought of to whom two of them belonged. His escape would be given an added relish because David Masefield Stewart had provided the means by which he carried it out. What was more, selling the pair and their saddles would—as he had not been paid by the rancher—help recompense him for what had otherwise proved a profitless affair.

Scanning his surroundings without seeing anything to disturb or alarm him the renegade again breathed a sigh of relief. It seemed either the Kid had been unable to locate him, or had gone to the jailhouse. In the latter case, having been told of the danger awaiting them should they come out, the men he had warned would be staying inside and letting the hired guns come in search of them.

Satisfied he had nothing more to fear, Corovan returned the Colt to his sash. Having done so, he walked forward confidently. While he still would need to make his escape from the town, he was feeling less qualms over this than he had a short while earlier. Compared with the Ysabel Kid, the hired guns from the Standing DMS ranch struck him as being as dangerous as the downtrodden squaw of a very strict Comanche warrior.

Such was the sense of elation relief was creating, as he was approaching the horses, the renegade looked at the store and wondered whether he should break in to see if anything was worth stealing before leaving Holbrock. Like most properties of its kind, its floor was raised a couple of feet from the ground in an attempt to deny entry to rodents wishing to feed upon its contents. Gaining admittance, therefore, would not be too difficult. However, as he had almost reached the elevated front veranda, he concluded the idea was not worth putting into effect. Wondering why no shots were fired, Leftie Scanlan might come, or send some of the "warriors" to investigate and they would make for the store.

Giving a shrug of resignation, Corovan went to the horses. As he reached for the reins of his mount, he was made aware that he was not alone at the building.

CHAPTER FIFTEEN

A:He; 'I Claim It'

NAMAE'ENUH!"

Even as the word came to his ears, although there had been not the slightest sound to explain how and from where the speaker had arrived, Dennis "Waxie" Corovan started to spin around. The employment of the far from flattering name given to the band of the Comanche nation to which his mother had belonged warned him that whoever had spoken must be well versed in *Nemenuh* lore. However, such was the state of alarm engendered by the voice, he did not give a thought to the insult. There was, he believed, only one person with the requisite knowledge and ability to approach him undetected in Holbrock.

The Ysabel Kid!

While turning rapidly, the renegade twisted his right hand around the walnut grips of his Colt 1860 Army revolver. Before it was clear of the sash, he saw somebody lunging his way who had—he suspected—been concealed beneath the veranda. With a sensation of horror so severe it caused him to freeze into immobility, he realized he had walked into a trap. One, moreover, which he ought to have anticipated when in contention against *Cuchilo*. Instead of having followed him, that god-damned *Pehnane* Dog Soldier had gambled upon him returning to collect his horse and had laid in ambush for him.

Even as his mind was drawing conclusions, when it would have been much better employed in directing motion to his limbs, the renegade saw a brief flicker which he knew to originate from the blade of a knife. Then he felt a sudden, yet not immediately painful sensation across the inside of his left thigh. An instant later, horror flooded through him as he guessed what had happened. Both the femoralis artery and the great saphenous vein had been severed, which meant he had only a very short time left to live.

Just as the realization struck home, another thought assailed Corovan. Vague though the figure of his assailant was in the darkness, he could make out certain physical features. They suggested he could be wrong in his assumption with regard to whom he was in contention against.

Firstly, although standing erect, the attacker was several inches shorter and lacked the whipcord slenderness of the Kid!

Secondly, the hair was much longer and held in a fashion which no Texas cowhand would have worn!

Thirdly, such a short and stocky build was typical of the Comanche nation!

All of which aroused, or rather clarified something which had been nagging at Corovan ever since he had fled from the alley. Although the Kid had undoubtedly been taught archery like every other potential brave-heart of the *Nemenuh* and might have kept in practice despite living so many years as a white man,[1] it was too great a coincidence that he would have anticipated the need and borrowed a bow and arrows from the *Kweharehnuh*.

Added together, the discoveries and final conclusion spelled one thing!

The mortal wound had not been delivered by the Ysabel Kid!

While Corovan had made the right revision where his assailant was concerned, he was not entirely correct with regards to the kind of person who had attacked him!

The wielder of the deadly knife was not of pure Comanche birthright!

---

1. *Proof that the Ysabel Kid had not forgotten his training at archery is given in:* RIO GUNS. *J.T.E.*

The injury was caused by one who the sycophant might have described as being another "white Indian!"

Acting as requested by the Kid, Annie Singing Bear had allowed José Salar and his five companions to pass un-impeded and without knowing of her presence. Then she had set off in search of the renegade responsible for the death of her favorite half brother, along with other of the *Pahuraix tuivitsi* he had led on a disastrous war trail. Having no liking for the towns of her maternal people, she had not gone into Holbrock to search for Corovan. Instead, after having kept watch from a nearby rim until she was con-vinced he was not there, she had made use of the information supplied by *Cuchilo* and had followed a couple of the hired guns to the Standing DMS ranch house. Taking even greater care than she had around the town, she had soon satisfied herself that the man she sought was on the premises. How-ever, even aided by the skills she had acquired to become a *tehnap,* she had been unable to approach close enough to carry out her lodge oath. Employing the patience which had been instilled in her by her upbringing, amongst other things living on pemmican and what small animals she could si-lently catch, she had remained in the vicinity to await an opportunity.

Seeing Salar return with one member of his party miss-ing, then set off again accompanied by six extra men, the girl had surmised that the attempt to catch up with and kill the Kid had failed. Satisfied she would be able to reach them and learn their intentions if she allowed them to get a moderate lead on her, she had decided to continue to keep the ranch house under observation for a short while longer. Watching the much larger party leave, including Corovan, she had changed her mind and followed them instead of the group with the Mexican.

It had proved a fortunate decision!

Guessing what was planned on seeing the renegade car-rying his Remington rifle and going with obvious reluctance into the town accompanied by two men, who looked more like guards than protectors, Annie had concluded she was being offered the opportunity she required. Arming herself with weapons that would allow her to kill more silently than was possible if she used her Winchester Model of 1866 carbine, she had left her two well trained horses hidden and followed on foot. Passing unseen by the "warriors" Wilson "Leftie" Scanlan had positioned ready to close in and attack the occupants of the jailhouse, she had watched the intended ambush prepared.

Despite having used her bow and arrows to kill the men with the renegade, the girl had had no intention of dealing with him in such a fashion. Instead, allowing him to take flight unharmed, she had gambled upon him returning to collect his horse once the first flood of panic had died away. Going to where it and the other two had been left, she had hidden beneath the veranda to await his arrival. When he had come, she launched her attack as her training as a Comanche warrior suggested would be best suited to her needs.

Spitting out a profanity as the understanding of the situation came to him, if not entirely correct on all points, Corovan tried to complete the drawing of the Colt and sucked in his breath to try and shout to Leftie Scanlan for help. Aware that he was dying and could not be saved, even by far greater medical skill and facilities than were available in the vicinity, he wanted to bring the segundo and hired guns into the town. By doing so, he hoped he would cause the death of at least some of the men he held responsible for his own forthcoming demise.

Drawing an accurate conclusion with regards to the motives of the mortally wounded renegade, Annie reacted with the deadly speed of a *Pahuraix tehnap*. Up and across lashed the J. Russell & Co. Green River hunting knife. This time, the razor sharp blade tore open his throat to sever his windpipe and vocal cords. An instant later, her other hand went to his chest and gave him a push which toppled him over backwards. On touching him with her palm she behaved as she had been taught was proper when tackling an enemy.

"A:he!" the word burst from the girl without the need for conscious thought.[2]

Unable to either cry out or fire the shot which could have started the gun battle he required, Corovan stared upwards at his assailant. He had already lost so much blood that movement was impossible. Despite his eyesight fading, he suddenly realized who it was standing over him. As was the case with the Kid, he had heard of Annie Singing Bear and her unconventional choice of life-style. As death claimed him, remembering the *Pahuraix tuivitsi* he had deserted to their fate when they had blundered into an ambush by soldiers of the United States' Cavalry, he knew why she had hunted him down and that she had fulfilled the lodge oath she had taken to avenge her half brother.

"May you go and rot in hell, you stinking Wormy 'mother-something!'" Annie hissed, as she gazed with mingled loathing and satisfaction at the man she had just killed, employing English as it offered a greater breadth of vocabulary with which to express her emotions. Reverting to Comanche, as she invariably thought in that language, she concluded just as quietly, "Now I'd better take a look at those other two, then let Magic Hands and Proud-Son-Of-Two-People know what's happening. After that, I'll go and help *Cuchilo.*"

"Town's quiet enough for a Sunday," Sheriff Dickson remarked, closing and bolting the front door of the jailhouse. He had just stepped outside to look and listen to what was happening in Holbrock, and heard nothing to disturb him. Walking across to the desk, he continued, "I know it's a touch early in the evening for anything to break loose, but I can't say I care much for the notion of you sitting in a room lit up like this after dark, Mort. Should they be so minded, it'd be real easy for somebody to sneak up and

2. A:he; *"I claim it:"* the declaration made by a Comanche warrior in a fight, when delivering a fatal blow or, regarded as more praiseworthy, touching an enemy with an empty hand, to announce he had "counted coup." J.T.E.

throw lead into you through one of the windows."

"Not happen you and Dusty've called it right and so long's I keep using *this* chair," Morton Lewis contradicted amiably, the peace officer having expressed similar misgivings on other occasions. Waving his left hand to where his big dog was lying close to the front entrance of the office, he went on, "Least-wise, not 'less they come sneaking along the sidewalk out there and figure on busting in on us. Which ole Pete's not about to let happen. 'Cording to you two officers 'n' gentlemen, sat right here, there's only the one place anywhere near's they can draw a bead on me from and either you or Dusty'll be headed off to keep watch on it now we've finished eating 'n' until I get bedded down for the night. 'Sides which, Stewart might want my spread and've counted on getting me hung so it'd come up for sale. But I don't reckon he'd be *loco* enough to have me gunned down cold-blooded in the jailhouse, even though those ya-hoos of his'n missed out on lynching me and trying to shoot me down 'legal-like' in here the day you brought me in."

"Stewart's not here," reminded Captain Dustine Edward Marsden "Dusty" Fog. "Sure I know we reckon Leftie Scanlan's only doing what he is to keep the good tax paying folks of Holbrook spooked and figuring maybe the scales of justice should ought to be tilted a mite the way his boss wants comes your trial. But some of those other guns Stewart hires might get ambitious and reckon on speeding things up a mite instead of waiting for the court to sit on you."

"That's what I was thinking," Dickson admitted. "Especially as they know the Kid's gone to see Chief Wolf Runner and can fetch back proof that will clear you."

Regardless of the comment he had just made, the sheriff was aware that allowing the rancher to be seen in the front office of the jailhouse was—while not without a certain amount of risk—far from being as foolhardy as might appear on the surface.

When deciding how best to safeguard Mort during the period of his protective custody, Dusty, Dickson and he had considered it unlikely any attempt upon his life would be made in the daytime, if at all. Despite the warnings passed by Leftie Scanlan, or rather at his instigation as he had not been into town since taking his injured cousin and Milton back to the DMS ranch house, there would be too many potential witnesses for him to chance anything illegal which could be seen and traced to him.

Regardless of their assumptions, the trio had next debated the merits of closing up the jailhouse completely—with the sturdy wooden shutters across the windows and both doors locked—from sundown to daybreak. After the small Texan and the sheriff had conducted a careful examination of the building and its surroundings, they had concluded that to take such measures offered more disadvantages than benefits. For one thing, despite there being observation slits with hinged covers on the inside in the doors and windows, viewing was restricted and closing the shutters would present a greater chance of men arriving outside without being detected. While of such sturdy construction the walls could only be breached by use of explosives, which would leave too much evidence of illicit activity for Scanlan to employ it, entry and exit by the occupants could be prevented.

Another point the trio had taken into consideration had been the effect of the precautions upon the people of the town. They had been made aware of Stewart's sentiments in the matter and were in something close to awe where the kind of men he hired was concerned. While much of the hostility against Mort had diminished, at the instigation of Brenton Humboldt, the people might consider that turning the jailhouse into something close to a fort was a sign of fear on the part of the sheriff. This in turn would increase the hold Scanlan could exert upon them.

With the latter point in mind, added to a desire to obtain evidence should Stewart have ordered Mort removed instead of waiting for a trial, it had been decided to follow what would appear to be a normal routine.

Using the absence of his two deputies as an excuse, Dickson had appointed the small Texan as a temporary replacement. Having eaten supper at the jailhouse, one of them would set out each evening ostensibly to make the rounds of the town. When certain he was not under observation, however, he would head for the alley which they had ascertained offered a limited view into the office such as was not granted anywhere else. With Mort willingly acting as bait, all possible precautions having been taken to keep him from harm, an ambush was laid for anybody sent to try and kill him from that point.

"Well, anyways," Dusty drawled, glancing at the clock on the wall. "It's time I took off to make sure nobody's figuring on making wolf bait of you."

The dryly spoken comment ended abruptly as the big dog raised its head and let out a low growl!

Coming swiftly to its feet, with hair bristling along the back, Pete loped swiftly through the open barred door giving access to the cell block at the rear of the building. Each drawing a revolver as he rose, the three men followed as quietly as possible. Without having made another sound, but still with the hair erect, the dog was sniffing at the back door. On a *sotto voce* word of command from its master, it sank into a crouch redolent of readiness to spring into immediate action if required.

"Who's there?" Dickson called, keeping out of the line of fire should shots come through the door as his companions were doing.

"Magic Hands, Proud-Son-Of-Two-People!" responded a feminine voice from outside the building. It spoke a tongue the sheriff did not know and, although recognizing the name he had been given by the Indians, Dusty only partially understood. "Let me in. I have much to tell and something to show you."

"It's Comanch' she's talking," the rancher informed, as the peace officer threw an interrogative glance his direction. "Only it's Water Horse and not Antelope like had she come from Grandpappy Wolf Runner." Then, raising his voice, he went on in the language of the *Nemenuh*. "It is far from the *tipis* of the *Pahuraix*, sister!"

"I know, I've rid' the son-of-a-bitch," the voice replied

in English. "Or do you reckon one of them fancy honky-tonk gals from the saloon's talking Comanch' to trick you into opening up?"

"I've never run across one of them who could," Mort claimed, quietly. "How about you, Dicks?"

"I can't even bring one to mind who looks part Indian," the sheriff admitted.

"Or me!" the rancher said pensively.

"Only?" Dusty prompted, having come to know Mort fairly well over the past few days of such close acquaintance.

"She talks Comanch' good enough to've been raised to it," the rancher obliged. "Only no *naivi*, nor *hervi*—which's a young gal, or woman growed to you white-eyes—is about to talk that sassy to a man, 'specially when she knows she's spouting it at one who rates's a name-warrior like Dusty and me do."

"Interesting" Dickson breathed.

"I'll go along with you on *that!*" the small Texan seconded. Fact being, I'd go so far as to say it could even be just a teensy mite *suspicious!*"

"Who are you, sister?" Mort challenged in his maternal tongue.

"Some call me 'Annie Singing Bear,'" the speaker outside answered, reverting to the same language. "But to my lodge brothers, I am 'Is-A-Man.'" Going back to English, she continued, "So how about opening up, *pronto."* "I've got news from *Cuchilo* and more, some of it I reckon the sheriff might not be liking over much."

"You can do it, Dicks!" the rancher authorized, duplicating the knowledge of the Kid where the girl to whom he was speaking was concerned. Feeling certain nobody at the Standing DMS ranch had sufficient contact with Comanche to have arranged such a bait for a trap, being unaware that Waxie Corovan had been there, he continued, "She's who and what she claims to be. Lie easy, you fool critter, she's not going to chomp, whomp, stomp, nor cook you, when she comes in."

"I hope he means that mangy old dog," Dusty said drily.

"So do I," the sheriff concurred and, still ensuring he was keeping the stone wall between himself and whoever was outside—a precaution which, despite having just guaranteed the *bona-fides* of the speaker, met with the approval of the rancher—he released the bolts. There was neither sting nor implied insult to the words as he went on while opening the door, "Anyways, *he's* the expert on Comanches. Come in, young lady."

The words were still being uttered when the girl crossed the threshold. Showing a shrewd tactical sense, she advanced swiftly until she too was sheltered by the wall and had allowed the door to be closed without any delay. Having carried out the first part of the plan she had elected to follow, she was holding more than her short and powerful bow, its quiver of arrows once more suspended on her back with the flights rising over her right shoulder. In her left hand, as well as two arrows which had clearly been removed from what was—or had recently been—living flesh, she grasped a Spencer repeating carbine.

"Howdy, gents," Annie greeted, her gaze resting for a moment on Dusty. However, regardless of the *Pahuraix* tending to be taller, she was sufficiently well acquainted with other Comanches to look beyond mere feet and inches, recognizing the true potential of "Magic Hands." You take chances, even for white-eyes. Three fellers just had it in mind to make wolf bait of Mort here."

"Well now," Dickson said quietly, his gaze going to the blood-smeared heads of the arrows to the face of their owner. "Seeing as it *didn't* happen, I'd say *something* must have happened to stop it."

"It did," the girl confirmed.

"You've only got *two* arrows there," the sheriff pointed out.

"Huh huh!" Annie grunted. "What I was after that dead faced son-of-a-bitch, Waxie Corovan for, I reckoned's how it was only right 'n' proper he should know from who and why he'd got it coming."

"I didn't hear any shooting," Dickson stated.

"Which's 'cause there wasn't none," the girl replied. "If you had, so would all those hired guns's're staked out every which way round this town of your'n ready to come in, heads down and horns a-hooking as soon's they heard guns play."

"I'll go close the shutters in the office, Dicks," Dusty offered, having returned his left hand Colt to the holster on the right side of his gunbelt—an action duplicated by his companions—when discovering it would not be needed. "Something tells me this young lady's going to be worth listening to."

"Hey, Mort," Annie remarked, nodding to where Pete was now lying in a relaxed posture. "I've heard tell about this dog of yourn'n, but damned if I ever believed it. Hell-on-wheels, *amigo*, all they said was *true*. He would be big enough to feed half a village, 'less he ate them all afore they could get him dressed for the pot."

"Us Antelopes raise 'em big and mean," the rancher answered with a grin, the comment by the girl having been worthy of a name-warrior from one band addressing a social equal belonging to another. "Let's go hear what you have to tell us, Is-A-Man."

CHAPTER SIXTEEN

High Odds, Even For *Cuchilo*

"Are you *sure* those three meant to kill Mort?" Sheriff Jerome Dickson inquired, after the party had returned to the now shuttered office of the jailhouse and the visitor had told what had happened outside.

"Well, I didn't go right on up and ask them was such their intentions," Annie Singing Bear replied. Despite realizing the peace officer was merely acting in accordance with how he would have performed his duty in other circumstances, she went on, "I can't claim to know a whole heap about how white folks think and do. But any time a Comanch' sees a feller lining a rifle, with two more jaspers backing him should anybody come around wanting to know what's doing, we sort of figure he's aiming to go shooting at *somebody*."

"I'd be like' to think on those lines myself," the sheriff admitted, although the way he ran his office had demanded the point be raised. "Was he going to do it with that Spencer?"

"Hell, no!" Annie denied. "He'd got him one of them Remington Army guns's'd throw a heap further and straighter than this. Only *Cuchilo* told me's how one'd been used to down those two fellers's Mort was blamed for dropping and I wondered, Spencers not being all that many around, was this the one's did it."

"It's worth looking into, Dicks," Captain Dustine Edward Marsden "Dusty" Fog commented. "I've heard there are ways to see whether a hull came from one gun or another and we've got the two empty cases you found at the Chass spread."

"I've heard the self-same thing," Dickson admitted, showing no resentment at the suggestion from the small Texan. "So maybe we'll get lucky when we take a—!" Noticing the girl was looking at a pot steaming on the stove, he paused, then asked, "When do you last eat, ma'am?"

"Around noon," Annie admitted.

"Can we offer you some of that stew?" the sheriff inquired. "We've all had our fill and there's plenty over."

"*Gracias,*" the girl assented. "I ran across *Cuchilo* on my way here, Cap'n Fog."

"Tell us about it while you're eating," Dusty advised with a smile. "Unless talking about him puts you off your food."

"It *won't!*" Annie declared vehemently, being very hungry. Then she adopted a more stoic attitude and continued, "Comes close to doing it, though."

Despite having a mutual interest in the welfare and doings of the Ysabel Kid, particularly so in the case of the small Texan because of their lengthy and very close association, none of the men pressed the girl for information while she was eating. After she had finished the liberal quantity of "son-of-a-bitch" stew—so called because, by tradition, the cook was expected to include whatever ingredients were available and boil them until, "you couldn't tell what any son-of-a-bitch he had used might be"—and was drinking a mug of coffee, she described her meeting with the Kid and the events which had led to it. Just as she was telling them about what she had seen and done when she and *Cuchilo* parted company, there was an interruption.

To the accompaniment of gun shots, the drumming of several sets of hooves approached hurriedly along the street and came to halt outside the building!

"Dickson!" called the voice of Wilson "Leftie" Scanlan. "Jerome Dickson, can you hear me in the jailhouse there?"

"I hear you," the sheriff admitted, seeing he was not alone in having drawn a revolver. "What do you want?"

"Mort Lewis!" the segundo replied. "He's gone way beyond just killing ole Dexter Chass 'n' his boy."

"We both know he never even got that far!" Dickson corrected. "He didn't do it and the Ysabel Kid's fetching back proof he couldn't have."

"I don't give a shit about what stinking pack of lies the Kid brings from that half breed bastard's kin!" Scanlan claimed. "Not since you let him out and he killed Cousin Slats and two of the Standing DMS hands and them without so much's a pocketknife 'tween them much less a gun—!"

"They'd got one gun at least!" the peace officer contradicted. "It's a Spencer that takes .52, Number 56 shells, like we found out to the Chass place. Which Mort's a .50, handling Number 52 cartridges."

"How much's the half breed paying you to come up with such a pack of lies?" the segundo demanded, after a pause to decide what to say. Silently cursing his dead cousin for having taken the Spencer carbine, the discovery that it was missing having caused him to pay the visit to the jailhouse, he went on, "'Cause, no matter how much, it's not going to save him now three of Mr. Stewart's men've been murdered by him. Comes noon tomorrow, me and every one of the crew're coming to take him from you 'n' see he gets what's coming to him."

"Nobody takes a prisoner from me!" Dickson stated, deciding his bluff with regards to the respective calibers proved the Spencer taken from Jacob "Slats" Scanlan was incriminating evidence.

"We aim to!" the segundo threatened, aware that the weapon would prove Morton Lewis innocent and might establish his own guilt of the double murder. "And don't count on getting any help from the folks in town. They'll know there's only two sides in this game, yours and Mr. Stewart's. Which, anybody's isn't for *him*, we'll just natural' conclude's an enemy and act accordingly."

"Which's against the law," Dickson warned.

"The law stops being the law when the bastard wearing the badge's taking bribes to stop a stinking half breed getting what's coming to him," Scanlan countered, knowing his words were being heard by more than just the occupants of

the jailhouse and confident they would soon be repeated all
through Holbrock. "There's nothing more to say, Dickson.
We'll be back comes noon tomorrow and we'll take your
half breed *friend* any way we have to."

"Sounded like he meant it!" Dusty remarked quietly, after
the rumbling of departing hooves had faded into the distance.

"That's what I thought," the sheriff replied, holstering
his revolver. "Let's hope the Kid gets back with that drawing
before noon!"

"Could be that feller out there's counting on him not
getting back at all," Annie suggested, replacing her cut down
Colt 1860 Army revolver. "I hadn't got around to mentioning it, but José Salar took off with ten hired guns and they
could only be fixing to stop him. Which's pretty high odds,
even for *Cuchilo*. Fact being, now I've give you the word,
I'm figuring on going to shorten them a mite."

"*Two* going would cut them same odds down *double*,"
Mort put in.

"You mean Dusty should ride with Annie?" Dickson inquired, but his tone held no suggestion of objecting to the
proposal.

"Not *Dusty*," the rancher corrected, hoping his motives
would be understood by the two men who had done so much
to help keep him alive. "Scanlan'll have men all around,
figuring to stop word getting out of what he's up to. Likely
even got the telegraph wires cut by now. Going out through
those yahoos's no chore for a paleface, even if he is 'Magic
hands.' Fact being, if the Kid's going to be sent help, the
only one's could get out and give it are a *couple* of what
that feller a few days back called 'white Indians.'"

"Sheriff Dickson, Captain Fog!"

"We hear you, Mr. Humboldt!" the peace officer replied,
recognizing the voice which called from among the crowd
gathered on the street outside the jailhouse about thirty minutes after the men from the Standing DMS ranch had taken
their departure. "Can we do something for you?"

"We heard what Scanlan told you," the banker declared. "So it's more the other way around. Can I come in and talk to you, please?"

"Come ahead," Dickson authorized, then glanced at the girl and went on *sotto voice*. "Go in the back out of sight, Annie!"

"Huh huh!" grunted the girl, picking up her bow and quiver—into which, after having cleaned the blood from them, she had returned the arrows used to kill Slats Scanlan and Moses "Bury 'Em" Milton—then obeying quickly.

"You win, blast it!" Dusty Fog drawled, sealing the envelope he had just addressed after inserting a letter he had written on paper also borrowed from the peace officer. "I was sure it'd take them at least forty-five minutes to come calling."

"It's what's known as local knowledge, *amigo*," Dickson answered, going to and unfastening the front door. Opening it while standing to one side, he continued, "Come ahead, Mr. Humboldt."

"You aren't going to hand Mr. Lewis over?" the banker said on entering, more as a statement than a question, clearly having come hurriedly from his home as he was wearing neither a cravat nor collar and the vest of his three piece suit was unbuttoned.

"I'm not," the sheriff confirmed.

"The County Commissioners support you in your decision," Humboldt stated.

"Unanimously?" Dickson inquired.

"Not in the first place," the banker admitted, still without so much as giving Dusty a glance. "But they all came around to m——We agreed in the end. So how can we help you, sheriff?"

"By staying at home tomorrow," the peace officer replied.

"Staying at *home?*" Humboldt challenged. "We mean to help you—!"

"That's the best way for you to do it," Dickson claimed. "Those men Scanlan'll have with him are hired guns—!"

"Several of us served in the late War, sir!" the banker interrupted, but there was a quiet dignity rather than pompous bombast in his voice. "Some not entirely without distinction."

"I'm not gainsaying that," the sheriff said, his tone friendly and respectful. "But the War's long over and not many of you have kept up your training in handling guns the way that'll be needed. On top of which, like I said, I'm not fetching Mort out to them. We're going to fort up in here and, should they want him bad enough to come against us; well, we're willing to let them try and take him."

"*Fort up* is the name for it!" Humboldt declared, glancing at the rack holding Winchester rifles and shotguns. Thinking of how sturdily the jailhouse had been constructed, he nodded and went on, "You have food, water, ammunition?"

"All we'll need," Dickson agreed. "Plenty to last us until the Kid gets back. Or to last out until those yahoos with Scanlan figure the game's gone sour and quit."

"I sent a telegraph message to a friend in Austin," the banker announced. "It got out before the wires went dead. He knows Stewart and will have it delivered."

"What did it say?" Dickson wanted to know.

"'If you want to stay out of jail, return immediately and control Scanlan,'" Humboldt explained. "I took the liberty of adding your name, sheriff and yours, Captain Fog."

"That's fine with me," the peace officer asserted and the small Texan gave his concurrence. "So, happen the push comes to a shove, all we need to do is fort up here and wait for Stewart to come running. He'll know what to expect should Scanlan be let play it through and soon enough call them off."

"That's what I thought," the banker admitted.

"Then you'll have everybody do as I ask?"

"You can count upon me to do my best to have them stay off the streets, sheriff!"

"Thanks, Mr. Humboldt," Dickson said with sincerity.

"It's the least I can do for Mr. Lewis," the banker replied. "After all, to a degree, I helped cause all this to happen.

You have my apologies, sir."

"Thank you, sir," the rancher replied and held out his right hand.

"Mr. Humboldt," Dusty drawled, after the two men had shaken hands and the banker was turning to leave. "Should it be *needed*, send this off to the General."

"I will," Humboldt promised, after holding the envelope he had been given for a couple of seconds and reading the address, "General J.B. Hardin, OD Connected, Rio Hondo County, Texas" in silence. "But I hope the need *doesn't* arise. And now, gentlemen, I'll bid you good night."

"You haven't had chance to see, or even talk about this scheme of his," Dickson remarked, after the banker had left and the door was secured.

"I don't need to," Dusty replied. "Uncle Devil's satisfied it will work and's worth investing in. It was Mr. Humboldt himself I'd been sent to see and talk to. There's some might say you'd talked a mite too much about *our* intentions, though. The word's sure to get back to Scanlan."

"That's what I'm counting on, the sheriff claimed, although he felt sure the explanation was unnecessary. "It'll give those yahoos backing him time to think on what they'll be facing when they come in tomorrow and, happen I know hired guns, some of them might even get to thinking the game's nowheres near stacked well enough in their favor, then pull out and look for safer work."

"Now might be a good time for Annie and me to get going," Mort remarked. "Or I could stay on and let her see what she can do for the Kid."

"You're *both* going," Dickson stated. "Should it be needed, the three of you coming in from back of them could turn things our way."

"Why sure," Dusty seconded. "Go do it, *amigo!*"

"I'll come let you out," the sheriff offered.

Going into the rear section with Mort, Dickson was grateful for the way in which it was laid out. Instead of being in the center, facing the main entrance, the back door was at the end of the row of cells. Therefore, it was left partially in shadows when the lamp hanging from the roof was turned down. While not entirely in darkness, it was sufficiently dim for their purpose.

"I'll go first," Annie offered as the men and the big dog joined her.

"Why *you?*" the rancher challenged.

"I'll be what you could call a 'surprise factor,'" the girl asserted. "Should they have somebody watching and I come up on him, I'll have a better chance of shutting his mouth than you would seeing's he won't know I'm in the game."

"Damned if I like to admit it, Is-A-Man," Mort declared. "But, just once in a while, you *Pahuraix* make good sense. Go get her done."

Accepting the rancher and girl knew what was best for their escape, Dickson unbolted and eased the back door open cautiously. As soon as it was wide enough for her to leave, Annie slipped through and faded as silently as a shadow into the darkness. However, before many seconds elapsed, there was a startled exclamation followed by a scuffling sound and the gasp of a human being in mortal pain.

"What the h—!" Dickson snapped, starting to open the door again. He had pushed it back nearly shut after the girl had left.

"Hold hard, Dicks!" Mort commanded, as the call of a whip-poor-will sounded from the same point that the brief and far from loud disturbance had originated. "Annie's all right and the way's cleared for us to get going."

"Now the Yankee rode down to the border,
Where he met an old pal, Bandy Parr,
Who run with the carpetbaggers,
And a meeting they held in a bar."

"He sure sings right pretty for a half breed," commented one of the Standing DMS ranch's hired guns, glancing to where José Salar was crouching at the other side of a bush. Then he turned his gaze to the bend in the trail through an area of fairly dense woodland where they and their companions were waiting to ambush the singer who was still out of sight. "I hope's he don't come 'round here too quick, seeing's how I've never heard that ole song all the way through."

Despite it appearing fortune was favoring him, the Mexican was less at ease than the man who had addressed him!

Ranging ahead of the "warriors" he had been given, Salar had seen a rider who he had identified as the Ysabel Kid!

While *Cabrito* had not changed into his all black clothing, the powder used to disguise his big white stallion had been cleaned away since the night of the abortive attempt to stop him at Sanchez Riley's trading post. Even as he had been seen over a rim, he had turned aside and made for the stage trail along which Mort Lewis had ridden after escaping from the jailhouse at Holbrock. By doing so, it had seemed he was playing into the hands of the men sent to get him.

There had been no discernible reason for the alteration in route!

As Salar had had barely more than his head and shoulders above the rim when he caught sight of *Cabrito*, stopping instantly he saw the other, he felt sure his presence had not caused the change. Nor had the Kid given even any slight indication of behaving in a more wary fashion. Instead, without even removing the buckskin pouch from the rifle across his bent left arm, he continued to hold the stallion to its leisurely seeming walk—which, nevertheless, covered a lot of ground at a fair speed—and remained slouching comfortably in the saddle to reduce the burden placed upon it.

Appreciating the chance he was being offered, the Mexican had hurried to rejoin his companions. He had also become aware of the difficulty of the task which lay ahead. To keep going was out of the question. Out in the open, so large a party could not hope to avoid being detected no matter how relaxed the Kid might be. When that happened, he would turn the stallion and make for a place of his own choosing to await their coming. Approaching him on such terms would be too perilous to be contemplated. With that in mind, Salar had decided they would return to the woodland and select a place from which to launch an ambush offering him no chance of escape.

Selecting the site had not been hard!

Choosing a straight length of the trail which would offer a good "killing ground," being hidden by a bend, the Mexican had divided the party. Leaving their horses some distance away and in concealment, they had taken up their positions on either side of the straight section. Nor had they been kept waiting for too long. Although he was still hidden from their view by the woodland, the Kid had been heard singing an old cowboy tune as he was riding towards them.

Regardless of the pleasant tenor voice implying their intended victim was in no way suspicious or expecting danger, Salar could not hold down the thought that such incautious behavior was not in keeping with all he had heard of the Ysabel Kid.

"Rosemary-Jo got word to her pappy,
He straddled his strawberry roan,
And said, 'From that ornery critter,
I'll save Rosemary-Jo, she's my own.'"

The next to last verse was coming from only a short way beyond the corner!

CHAPTER SEVENTEEN

This We Didn't Count On

"Now the Yankee lit out for Dallas,
Met the Texan out on the square,
His draw was too slow and as far as I know,
That Yankee's still laying out—!"

Listening to the final verse of the song, the hired gun crouching next to José Salar began to rise and bring the butt of his Henry rifle to his shoulder. Taking sight to where their intended victim would appear, he decided he was going to be fortunate enough to hear the "Rosemary-Jo Lament" all the way through and hoped none of the other hired guns covering the trail would open fire before he was given the opportunity.

With the words still continuing, the magnificent white stallion appeared, walking slowly, around the bend!

Although the pleasant tenor voice was reaching their ears, the waiting "warriors" were given a shock!

The big horse was not carrying a rider!

Having evaded his pursuers at Sanchez Riley's trading post, there had only been one untoward event before the Ysabel Kid reached the village of the *Kweharehnuh* Comanche. Seen by a small party of warriors, he was compelled to cope with an attack by the *tuivitsi* who had collected the Sharps New Model of 1866 rifle on the day of the buffalo hunt. Dealing with this, less violently than might have been the case, his medicine pouch had been enough to allow him to explain his business. Escorted to meet Chief Wolf Runner, he had described his meeting with Morton Lewis and what had happened subsequently. Receiving the drawing produced by Geraldine Thatcher, he had remained at the village for long enough to allow the stallion to rest and, its disguise removed as no longer necessary, he had set out on the return journey.

Under the prevailing conditions, no *Pehnane* Dog Soldier ever traveled in an incautious fashion no matter how he appeared externally and, white man's clothing notwithstanding, the slender Texan came into such a category when danger threatened.

Keeping a far better watch than had appeared to be the case, a brief glint from the sun off one of the silver *conchas* decorating the band of the Mexican's *sombrero* had given a warning to the Kid. Feeling sure Salar was not alone and might even have obtained reinforcements, he had thought quickly and decided what would be his best course of action against them. Possessing the excellent retentive memory of a Comanche, particularly with regards to the geography of any terrain he had recently traversed, he had known he must pass through the woodland to reach Holbrock. With that in mind, guessing how the Mexican would react, he had set about arranging to meet them on his own terms and at a place, if not entirely of his own choosing, somewhat suited to his purpose.

Turning towards the trail, the Kid had ridden along it into the woodland. Although prior to entering the wood he had not come across any evidence to show he was correct in his assumption, there were sufficient indications to his animal-wise senses to suggest that Salar was acting as anticipated. Therefore, as he was approaching the area which he had instinctively selected while passing through in the other direction as being an excellent point for an ambush, he had ridden along singing to lull the men he thought would be waiting into a sense of false security. Just before reaching the bend around which he believed they were waiting, he had dropped from the saddle—having removed the medicine pouch from his Winchester Model of 1866 rifle and tucked it beneath the cantle—allowing Blackie to walk onwards while he darted into the undergrowth at the side of the trail. Using his voice in the close to ventriloquial fashion he had been taught as a child, he had conveyed the impression that he was still riding.

Even as the waiting "warriors" realized they had been tricked, a shrill whistle sounded from amongst the bushes. Instantly, the stallion changed its leisurely walking gait and built up to a gallop along the trail. Seeing what he considered to be such a valuable and desirable a piece of loot approaching, the last of the men on the left side put down his rifle and ran forward to acquire it. Such an action, as anybody who knew Blackie could have warned, was most ill-advised. Letting out a savage snorting squeal, the big white charged. Thrusting forward its neck, it seized him with its jaws and, a hackamore being used, there was no bit to prevent the mouth closing upon his shoulder. Grasped with such force, pain numbed his senses, he was flung backwards to the ground. An instant later, the stallion's slashing iron shod hooves were battering the life from him. Spluttering out an alarmed profanity, another of the hired guns brought up his rifle with the intention of killing the raging animal.

"He's tricked u——!" the "warrior" next to Salar began.

From the other side of the trail, a Winchester cracked. Hit in the head, the man died without having quite achieved his ambition of hearing "that ole song" all the way through.

Having seen and disposed of the first of his intended killers, the Kid swivelled as he was throwing the lever through its reloading cycle. The nearest of the "warriors" on the same side of the trail was rising from behind a fallen tree trunk and turning his way. Already cradled at the right shoulder, the "ole yellow boy" seemed to halt and fire of its own volition when pointing in the required direction. Caught in the chest before he could attain a firing position, the man spun around and disappeared once more.

However, despite becoming aware of the threat to his horse, a bullet from a repeating rifle closer to hand caused the Kid to give his attention to the man who had fired at him. Even as he was preventing the owner of the Henry from improving its aim, he was bitterly aware that he could not hope to do so and turn the Winchester quickly enough to save Blackie. Nor, offered so large a target, was the "warrior" further along the trail likely to miss.

Lining his rifle at the stallion as it was stamping the other hired gun to death, the would-be avenger heard a rushing patter of some kind of four-footed creature approaching from his rear. Before he could turn to investigate, there was a roaring snarl and he was struck on the back with such force by a heaving and living weight he was sent sprawling, the rifle flying from his grasp. Landing face down with the animal on top of him, he gave a surging heave and rolled over. This proved a fatal error. Leaping clear, the big shaggy coated dog which felled him lunged and caught him by the throat. Powered by the jaws, the teeth sank onwards and, with the head shaking, worried at the neck with deadly efficiency.

Hooves rumbled in the woodland and two riders dashed from the same direction as the dog had appeared!

Having made good their departure from Holbrock the previous night, Annie Singing Bear and Morton Lewis, using her horses, had detected the ambush as they were following the route they hoped would take them to the Kid. Hearing him singing, they had shown greater perception than the men lying in wait. Waiting until the appropriate moment, having sent Pete to save the white stallion, they were now taking cards in the deadly game.

Showing the skill of his Camanche upbringing, the rancher was guiding his borrowed mount by knee pressure alone. Aiming his Spencer carbine and without slowing down he sent one of the hired guns tumbling lifeless to the ground. Displaying an equal ability, the girl used her Winchester to just as lethal effect against another of the Standing DMS hired guns.

"It's Dusty Fog and the sheriff!" yelled a "warrior" on the same side of the trail as Salar and turned to run.

No coward, neither was the Mexican a fool. Realizing the ambush had gone terribly wrong, he did not intend to wait to discover whether the speaker was correct in identifying the newcomers. It was obvious, no matter who they might be, they had evaded Wilson "Leftie" Scanlan and the rest of the crew. Which meant they were fighters of greater than average ability. Given their backing, staying to face _Cabrito_ would be the equivalent of committing suicide. Reaching that conclusion, Salar swung around without attempting to use his Sharps rifle. He and the "warrior" who had spoken started to make for the horses.

When the Kid saw the Mexican was leaving, he set off in pursuit. Two bullets came his way as he was crossing the trail, but missed due to the speed at which he was moving. When he saw that the man who shot first was close enough to be dangerous, and appeared determined to try again, he began to fire the Winchester on the run. Making the most of its capacity for rapid operation, although not quite attaining the possible two shots per second, he sent a spray of lead which engulfed the "warrior." Just as the man was sent down, he felt the lever stick on a half closed position and knew the mechanism was suffering from a flaw in its design. Even if there was time, he did not have the means with him to repair the broken toggle link.[1]

Tossing the temporarily useless rifle into a bush as he passed, the Kid returned his right hand palm outwards to twist the heavy old Colt Dragoon revolver from its holster.

Following the fleeing Mexican, aware of his limitations with the weighty weapon, the Kid did not attempt to use it as a means of ending the flight. However, hearing a disturbance in the undergrowth as the horses were coming into view, he glanced to find the final pair of hired guns were approaching. Although they too had escape in mind, the sight of him provoked hostile reactions. Skidding to a turning halt facing them, he crouched and began to fire at waist level by instinctive alignment. Shot after shot left the four

---

1. _Further information regarding this defect in the Winchester Model of 1866 and how it could be repaired is given in:_ CALAMITY SPELLS TROUBLE. _J.T.E._

pounds, one ounce, thumb-busting old revolver. Smoke from the massive powder charge in each chamber of the cylinder swirled from the muzzle to make him an elusive target at which to aim in return and this was the effect he sought.

One of the men screamed as he took a .44 caliber soft lead ball in the right shoulder and was hurled from his feet with an arm he would never use again. An instant later, just as he was satisfied with his aim at the vague figure beyond the gaseous cloud, the second hired gun was felled by bullets from the Winchester carbine and Spencer of the other two "white Indians" who had crossed the path to take part in the pursuit.

Realizing yet another potential danger was ended, the Kid raced onwards. Unsure exactly how many times he had fired, which was excusable under the circumstances, he was disinclined to rely upon there being loaded chambers. Dropping the revolver, he reached across to bring the massive James Black bowie knife from its sheath.

"*Pelado!*"

At the shouted word, meaning a corpse or grave robber of the vilest kind in the Spanish spoken along the bloody border between Texas and Mexico, Salar turned from the horse he had been unfastening. Seeing the Kid rushing towards him, he brought up and aimed the Sharps. Excellent though it undoubtedly was for accuracy at long distances, it was much less suitable for fast work at close quarters. With the sights aligned on the chest and right forefinger squeezing the trigger, he watched his intended target suddenly commence a rolling dive. Unable to alter the direction of the barrel or halt the pressure, he fired and knew he had missed.

Alarm flooded through the Mexican!

About to drop the now empty rifle and draw his Colt, the chance was not presented for Salar to do so!

Ending the roll in a kneeling posture, the Kid swung his right arm in a swift horizontal arc. Passing just above the waist belt, the razor sharp edge of the bowie knife's blade sliced through the white silk shirt and bit onwards deep into the flesh below. It ripped across the width of the lower torso like red hot steel passing through butter. Unable to cry out, Salar túrned involuntarily away. The Sharps slipped from his grasp and his hands went to where the intestines were flooding out of the mortal wound. Buckling at the knees, he toppled dying to the ground.

"Aihe!" grunted the Kid, as much a Comanche as "Is-A-Man" had been when counting coup upon Dennis "Waxie" Corovan in Holbrock.

"Are you all right, *Cuchilo?"* Annie asked, reining her horse to a halt.

"Yes," the Kid replied. "How about them?"

"If any are still alive, they're running!" Mort claimed. "Let's go and get those fools critters of ours back, shall we, *Cuchilo?"*

"Be be—!" the Kid began, but was interrupted by the sound of many hooves approaching from the direction he had come. Looking at the riders galloping through the woodland, he went on, "Well I'll be damned. I didn't know either of them were hereabouts!"

"You in the jailhouse! Can you hear me?" Leftie Scanlan yelled. "I got your word, but it's not going to work. I've got Banker Humboldt out here with a gun to his head. If you don't fetch out the half breed and hand him over, I'm going to find out if he really does have dollar bills instead of brains!"

"He has got Humboldt!" Captain Dustine Edward Marsden "Dusty" Fog confirmed, having crossed the office to raise the cover and look out of a loophole in the shutter of a window. "This we didn't count on!"

"I don't reckon he'd be *loco* enough to do it," commented Sheriff Jerome Dickson, coming from where he had been keeping watch at the rear.

"Or me," the small Texan admitted. "But can we take a chance on it?"

The clock on the wall of the office had just struck noon!

Ever since daybreak, the main street of Holbrock had resembled a ghost town!

At the request of Brenton Humboldt, passed around the previous evening as he had promised, the citizens had remained in their homes, keeping their children inside and leaving their businesses closed!

Following the plan outlined by Dickson, he and Dusty had not been outside the jailhouse. Closed shutters protected the windows and the two doors were secured by locks and bolts. Although neither had believed an attack would be launched when the segundo of the Standing DMS ranch saw they had done as announced, they had fully loaded every firearm on the premises and were prepared for defense or a siege.

From what they had just heard, the small Texan and the peace officer realized their intentions were being thwarted in a way neither had envisaged!

Opening the loophole in the other window, Dickson joined Dusty in studying the situation!

Neither under-estimated its extreme gravity!

Instead of having ridden to where the street broadened to form what amounted to a small *plaza* in front of the jailhouse, or approaching on foot along the sidewalk—perhaps with others closing in at the rear—Scanlan had brought his men so they had given little indication of their coming. They now formed a half circle in the square. Some were watching the building with rifles in their hands. The rest faced and were menacing the townsmen who were gathering beyond them.

However, to the watchers in the office, the most important sight was proof that Scanlan could do as he threatened!

Standing in the center of his men, the segundo was holding Humboldt as Mort Lewis had on the day of the flight from the jailhouse. There was, as Dusty and Dickson were aware, one very great difference. The rancher would have been unlikely to use the revolver menacing the banker. Each knew they could not rely upon Scanlan to show a similar reluctance. At least, neither was sufficiently confident in their belief to put Humboldt's life at risk by resisting when the segundo called for them to "come out of there and bring the half breed with you."

"We're coming," the sheriff called, glancing at the sawed off shotgun he was holding, then nodding at his companion.

"There're times I wish I'd led a better life," Dusty drawled, leaning his Winchester carbine against the wall to unfasten the door. Leaving the saddlegun where it was, he continued as he started to open the door. "And *this* could be one of them!"

"I know how you feel," Dickson admitted and led the way from the jailhouse.

"I don't see the half breed with you!" Scanlan growled, as the two men advanced and stopped at the edge of the sidewalk twenty feet from where he and the banker were standing.

"You didn't expect to," Dickson stated, keeping the shotgun held in front of him and down at arms' length. "After last night, you *know* he's not here."

"The hell he's not!" the segundo denied. "That big claybank of his's still down to the livery barn. We'd have heard him had he rid'out on something else and he sure as shit hasn't gone on foot."

"How about that man of yours you found out back?" Dickson challenged.

"Sure we found Joe knife-ripped and wolf bait," Scanlan admitted. "But the Ysabel Kid must've got by Salar and his bunch, then done it coming in."

"It was Mort Lewis going out," the sheriff corrected, if inaccurately. "I turned him loose so you couldn't get your lousy hands on him."

"If you did, you're going to regret it," the segundo declared. "I've promised these good folks a hanging and I don't aim to disappoint them. Turning a murderer loose makes you an accessory to his killings, which rates a rope in my book."

"So you figure on hanging the sheriff?" Dusty asked.

having allowed his companion do the talking as a matter of courtesy.

"And you 'n' that black dressed 'breed you brought," Scanlan replied. "You're in it with Dickson from soda to hock."

"Do you think you can do it?" the small Texan inquired, voice as gentle as the first stirrings of a summer whirlwind.

"Do *you* reckon I can't?" the segundo challenged, gouging with his left hand Remington into the banker's throat. "'Cause, happen you do, ask Humboldt here what *he* reckons about it."

"Don't give in to him!" the banker ordered, face flushed with outrage over having been dragged from his home at gun point and used in such a fashion.

"Scanlan!"

Having been allowed to pass between two of the hired guns—who knew him to be a supporter of their employer—holding a revolver in his hand, the member of the posse with whose wife the segundo was having an affair called the name as he walked forward.

"Yeah?" Scanlan grunted, eyeing the speaker disdainfully.

"Martha's told me what's going on between you!"

"So?"

"So I'm going to kill you!" the man declared and started to raise his weapon.

The betrayed husband was being far less reckless than he seemed. Nor was he acting on any spur of the moment impulse. Having suspected what was happening between his wife and Scanlan, due to hints given by neighbors, he had beaten the truth out of her that morning. This had been accompanied by a threat of vengeance on her lover. Locking her in a room at home, he had joined the crowd hoping to find some way of avoiding the reprisals. Being quick witted in some matters, he had seen what he believed opened a way which would have the added advantage of earning public acclaim and the possibility of patronage from the banker.

"Get the hell away from here, you stupid bastard!" the segundo snarled, realizing he was exposed to the gun of a man less likely to care than either the sheriff or the small Texan for the well being of Humboldt.

Regardless of his belief that the betrayed husband lacked the guts to do more than threaten, Scanlan could not prevent himself relaxing the hold of his right hand and moving the Remington from beneath his captive's chin. Making the most of the opportunity, Humboldt jerked free his neck and rammed his right elbow to the rear. As it struck and pushed the segundo away, he jumped aside.

Alert for any way out of the predicament, Dickson began to raise his shotgun!

Swiftly though the sheriff moved, Dusty Fog proved *much* faster!

Crossing, the small Texan's hands grasped the bone grips and swept the Colt 1860 Army reolvers from their carefully designed holsters. Such was his completely ambidextrous prowess, cocked and ready by the time their barrels were turned to the front, they roared at practically the same instant and slightly over half a second after the commencement of the draw. The two .44 caliber bullets entered Scanlan's left breast less than three inches apart, sending him backwards and causing his Remington to discharge harmlessly into the air.

In echo to the cracks from the Colts, the sheriff changed the aim of his weapon and threw nine .32 buckshot balls into a "warrior" who was showing signs of aggression!

A moment later, the top of his skull bursting open and spinning his hat into the air under the impact of a bullet of heavy caliber, another of the Standing DMS ranch's hired guns was thrown from his feet as he tried to raise his rifle.

The shot had not been fired from within the town!

Turning his gaze to where the boom of a rifle sounded, one of the "warriors' gave a yell of alarm. Looking in the direction he was indicating, the rest shared his consternation. Nor were many of the assembled townsmen less perturbed to see the rim—from which Annie Singing Bear had conducted her surveillance when looking for Corovan—was lined with well armed Indians. Sitting his horse between Chief Wolf Runner and a stocky, bearded white man whose most prominent piece of cowhand attire was a vest made from the hide of a jaguar, another elderly Comanche with the flowing "war bonnet" denoting high social standing was ejecting the spent cartridge case from a Sharps rifle. Although of *Nemenuh* style and manufacture, none of his garments were made from pronghorn hide.

Riding down the slope at a gallop, Winchesters and Spencer carbine held ready to be used, were the Ysabel Kid, Morton Lewis and the "surprise factor" who had led Scanlan to form an erroneous conclusion about the killing of the "warrior" the previous night, Annie Singing Bear.

"Give it up, you men!" Dickson commanded. "Those *Kweharehnuh* won't hurt the town people, but they'll take the hair from every god-damned Standing DMS son-of-a-bitch who doesn't yell 'calf rope' and fast!"

"Scanlan wasn't following Stewart's orders on this!" Dusty supplemented from behind his recocked Colts, drawing an accurate conclusion with regards to the motives of the segundo; whose intention had been to have the sheriff and Mort killed, presenting his employer with a *fait accompli* where the ambition to gain control of the whole region was concerned. "You'll get no pay from him!"

"Can you keep those red bastards from butchering us?" asked one of the hired guns and the others muttered a desire to be given an answer.

"The Kid and Mort can, happen they've a mind," the sheriff replied. "Which they will have, if you give it up."

"What'll you do to us?" the "warrior" wanted to know.

"Nothing," Dickson promised. "Just so long as you get the hell clear out of Holbrock County and don't *ever* come back!"

"Captain Fog!" the sycophant said, coming over after the hired guns had taken their depature. Having noticed a certain coolness towards him from Humboldt, he was seeking to make amends for whatever might have caused it. "I am giving a dinner party for Brenton and his family to celebrate his fortunate escape. Would you care to be my guest at it?"

"Why thank you, sir," Dusty replied, then glanced to the three "white Indians" who were standing near by. "Will Annie, Mort and Lon be coming?"

"Well—!" the man said hesitantly. "I'm sure Mr. Lewis and the young wo—er—*lady* have other things they want to do, but your man can come with you."

"Why thank you 'most to death, sir," the Kid drawled, in his most innocent fashion. Looking to where the reinforcements who had joined his party at the place of the ambush were still sitting their horses, he went on, "Reckon it'd be all right was I to fetch my grandpappy along?"

"Grand—?" the sycophant commenced, also turning his gaze to the rim. "If you wish to. He probably doesn't feel at ease with all those Indians."

"Why wouldn't he?" the Kid inquired, despite guessing the answer.

"Well," the man explained, being willing to show a sociable spirit to the slender Texan in order to ingratiate himself with Dusty Fog. "A white man *wouldn't* be surrounded by so many Indians."

"*White man?*" the Kid drawled in apparent puzzlement. Then, nodding as if understanding had suddenly come, he went on, "Hell, that's Colonel Charlie Goodnight.[2] But he's Dusty's kin not mine."

"*Not yours?*" queried the sycophant.

"Shucks, no," the Kid confirmed, his tone mocking and sardonic. Raising his right hand to give a wave to which the elderly Comanche holding the Sharps rifle responded in

---

2. *Chief Long Walker had come from the* Pehnane *Comanche reservation accompanied by his good friend, Colonel Charles Goodnight to help his grandson keep the* Kweharehnuh *from taking the war path. Arriving shortly after the Ysabel Kid had set out from the village, they had followed with Chief Wolf Runner and a number of braves to lend moral support if it should be needed.*

the same manner, he concluded, "That's *my* grandpappy, Chief Long Walker of the *Pehnane*, up there on the rim. See, mister, I'm what *you*'d call a 'White Indian' myself."[3]

3. *David Masefield Stewart never returned to the Standing DMS ranch, or Holbrock County. Receiving a warning of what had happened from one of his supporters while on his way from Austin, he fled from Texas and sold his ranch to a wealthy Easterner who proved to be a less ambitious and more friendly neighbor to Morton Lewis. J.T.E.*

In Conclusion

Having read the Berkley Books, February, 1981, U.S.A. edition of THE HALF BREED—which, for some unaccountable reason, we have never supplied to Alvin Dustine "Cap" Fog in any of its editions by Corgi Books—he sent the added information which has provided the basis for this book and asked if we would give precedence to producing this "expansion."

Cap said that, as it has become the habit in "liberal" movies and television shows to portray any successful businessman whose efforts and efficiency have proved beneficial to the economy of the United States of America as a criminally inclined, grasping, corrupt and immoral bigot, he felt we should make amends to the memory of Brenton Humboldt and we were only too willing to do so.

Appendix One

Soon after his enrollment in the Army of the Confederate States,[1] Dustine Edward Marsden "Dusty" Fog had won promotion in the field to captain before he was seventeen years of age and was put in command of the Texas Light Cavalry's hard riding, harder-fighting Company "C."[2] Leading them throughout the campaign in Arkansas, he had earned the reputation for being an exceptionally capable military raider and a worthy, if junior, contemporary of the South's other leading exponent of what eventually became known as "commando" tactics,[3] Turner Ashby and John Singleton "the Grey Ghost" Mosby.[4] In addition to his other exploits, he had prevented a pair of pro-Union fanatics from starting an Indian uprising which would have decimated much of Texas,[5] and supported Belle "the Rebel Spy" Boyd on two of her most dangerous assignments.[6]

At the conclusion of the War Between The States, Dusty became *segundo* of the great OD Connected ranch in Rio Hondo County, Texas. Its owner and his paternal uncle, General Jackson Baines "Ole Devil" Hardin, C.S.A.,[7] had been crippled in a riding accident,[8] which placed much added responsibility on Dusty's young shoulders. This included handling an important mission upon which the future relations between the United States of America and Mexico hung in the balance.[9] While doing so, he was helped by two men who became his closest friends and leading lights in the ranch's floating outfit,[10] Mark Counter[11] and the Ysabel Kid. Aided by them, he had helped gather horses to replenish the war-reduced *remuda* of the OD Connected, [12] then was sent to assist Colonel Charles Goodnight[13] on the trail drive to Fort Sumner, New Mexico,[14] which had done much to help the Lone Star State recover from the improverished conditions left by its support of the ill fated Confederate cause. With that accomplished, he was equally successful in helping Goodnight convince other ranchers it would be possible to drive large herds of half wild longhorn cattle to the markets offered by the railroads passing through Kansas.[15]

Having proven himself a first class cowhand, Dusty went on to earn fame as a very competent trail boss,[16] a roundup captain,[17] and a town taming peace officer.[18]. Competing in the revolver handling competition at the first Cochise County Fair, he won the title, "The Fastest Gun In The West," by beating a number of well-known exponents of rapid gun handling and accurate shooting.[19] In later years, following his marriage to Lady Winifred Amelia "Freddie Woods" Besgrove-Woodstole,[20] he became a noted diplomat.

Dusty never found his lack of stature an impediment to his achievements. In addition to being naturally strong,[21] he had taught himself to be completely ambidextrous.[22] Possessing perfectly attuned reflexes, he could draw either, or both, his Colts—no matter whether the 1860 Army Model,[23] or their improved successors, the 1873 Single Action Army Model[24]—with lightning speed, and could shoot very accurately. Ole Devil's "valet," Tommy Okasi,[25] was Japanese and a trained *samaurai*.[26] From him, along with the General's "granddaughter" Elizabeth 'Betty' Hardin,[27] the small Texan had been taught *ju jitsu* and *karate,* neither of which form of unarmed combat had received the publicity they would later be given, they were little known in the Western Hemisphere at that time. Therefore, Dusty found the knowledge a very useful surprise factor when he had to fight barehanded against larger, heavier and stronger men.

1. *Details of some of the career of Dustine Edward Marsden "Dusty" Fog prior to his enrollment are given in:* Part Five, the Civil War series, "A Time For Improvization, Mr. Blaze," J.T.'S HUNDREDTH.

2. *Told in:* YOU'RE IN COMMAND NOW, MR. FOG.

3. *The first "commandos" were bands of South African irregular troops fighting very successfully against the British Army in the Boer War.*

4. *Told in:* THE BIG GUN, A MATTER OF HONOR, UNDER THE STARS AND BARS *and* KILL DUSTY FOG!

5. *Told in:* THE BIG GUN

6. *Told in:* THE COLT AND THE SABER *and* THE REBEL SPY. *Other episodes of the life of Belle "the Rebel spy" Boyd are recorded in:* A MATTER OF HONOR, THE BLOODY BORDER, BACK TO THE BLOODY BORDER, THE HOODED RIDERS, THE BAD BUNCH, TO ARMS! TO ARMS! IN DIXIE!, THE SOUTH WILL RISE AGAIN, THE QUEST FOR BOWIE'S BLADE, Part Eight, "Affair of Honor," J.T.'S HUNDREDTH, THE REMITTANCE KID, THE WHIP AND THE WAR LANCE *and* Part Five, "The Butcher's Fiery End," J.T.'S LADIES.

7. *Details of the career of General Jackson Baines "Ole Devil" Hardin, C.S.A., can be found in the* Ole Devil Hardin *series;* Part Four, "Mr. Colt's Revolving Cylinder Pistol," J.T.'S HUNDREDTH—*covering his early life—the* Civil War *and* Floating Outfit *series and his death is reported in:* DOC LEROY, M.D. *The General's sobriquet arose partly as a result of his deliberately enhancing the Mephistophelian aspects of his features when he was younger and because his contemporaries claimed he was a "lil ole devil for a fight."*

8. *Told in:* Part Three, "The Paint," THE FASTEST GUN IN TEXAS.

9. *Told in:* THE YSABEL KID. (*When sent as a manuscript to our first publishers, Wagon Wheel Westerns, in 1961, we gave it the title,* DUSTY FOG, *but it was changed by the editor without consulting us.*)

10. *"Floating outfit:" four to six cowhands employed on a large ranch to work the more distant regions of the property. Taking food and other necessities in a chuck wagon or "greasy sack" on the back of a mule, they would be away from the ranch house for long periods and so were the pick of the crew. Because of General Hardin's prominence in the affairs of Texas, the floating outfit of the OD Connected ranch were frequently dispatched to assist such of his friends who found themselves in serious difficulties or danger.*

11. *Details of the career and special qualifications of Mark Counter can be found in* Part Two, "We Hang Horse Thieves High" J.T.'S HUNDREDTH *and various volumes of the* Floating Outfit *series.*

12. *Told in:* .44 CALIBER MAN *and* A HORSE CALLED MOGOLLON.

13. *The military rank, "Colonel," granted to Charles Goodnight was honorary and out of respect for his abilities as a fighting man and leader. As is recorded in the* Alvin Dustine "Cap" Fog *series, Dusty Fog was accorded a similar honor later in his life.*

14. *Told in:* GOODNIGHT'S DREAM (*Bantam Books, U.S.A., 1974*

edition retitled, THE FLOATING OUTFIT, *although there is an entirely different Corgi Books edition with that title) and* FROM HIDE AND HORN.

15. *Told in:* SET TEXAS BACK ON HER FEET *(Although Berkley Books' first U.S.A. edition was re-titled,* VIRIDIAN'S TRAIL, *they subsequently reverted to the original title).*

16. *Told in:* TRAIL BOSS *(Our first published work).*

17. *Told in:* THE MAN FROM TEXAS *(Our original recommendations to Sabre Books was far more suitable in our opinion, if not that of the editor,* ROUNDUP CAPTAIN.)

18. *Told in:* QUIET TOWN, THE MAKING OF A LAWMAN, THE TROUBLE BUSTERS, THE GENTLE GIANT, THE SMALL TEXAN *and* THE TOWN TAMERS.

19. *Told in:* GUN WIZARD.

20. *The members of the Hardin, Fog and Blaze clan with whom we have consulted decline to explain why Lady Winifred Amelia "Freddie Woods" Besgrove-Woodstole decided to leave England and live under an assumed name in the United States of America. Nor was a present day member of the Besgrove-Woodstole family, the Right Hon. Brenda— who makes a "guest" appearance in* THE LAWMEN OF ROCKABYE COUNTY—*wife of Sheriff Jack Tragg, any more inclined to be informative.*

21. *One example of Dusty Fog exhibiting his exceptional muscular physique and strength is given in:* MASTER OF TRIGGERNOMETRY, *the "expansion" of Part One, "The Schoolteacher,"* THE HARD RIDERS.

22. *The ambidextrous prowess was in part hereditary. It was possessed and exploited just as effectively by the grandson of Freddie and Dusty, Alvin Dustine "Cap" Fog, q.v. "Cap" also inherited the physique of a Hercules in miniature and these traits helped him to become, in addition to arguably the greatest combat pistol handler of his generation, the youngest man ever to hold rank of captain in the Texas Rangers. However, some authorities award the "combat pistol" honor to Ed. McGivern, author of,* FAST AND FANCY REVOLVER SHOOTING, *a partly autobiographical work and a definitive treatise upon the subject.*

23. *Although the military sometimes claimed derisively it was harder to kill a soldier than a sailor, the weight factor of the respective weapons caused the United States' Navy to adopt a revolver of .36 caliber and the Army settled for the heavier .44. The weapon would be carried on the belt of a seaman and not—handguns having originally and primarily been developed for use by cavalry—upon the person or saddle of a man who would be doing much of his traveling and fighting on the back of a horse. Therefore, by tradition, .44 became classified as the 'Army' caliber and .36 the 'Navy.'*

24. *Information regarding the Colt Model P "Single Action Army" revolver is given in those volumes of the* Floating Outfit *series which come after* THE PEACEMAKERS *on the chronological list.*

25. *"Tommy Okasi" is an Americanized corruption of the name given by the man in question when he was rescued from a derelict vessel in the China Sea by a ship under the command of General Hardin's father. Due to the families involved, who have living descendants holding positions of importance in Japan, the Hardin, Fog and Blaze clan consider it inadvisable even at this late date to disclose why Tommy had to leave his native land.*

26. *"Samaurai:" a member of the Japanese nobility's elite warrior class who usually served as retainers for the Daimyos, the hereditary feudal barons. A masterless samaurai who became a mercenary was known as a ronin. From the mid-1870's, increased contact with the Western Hemisphere brought an ever growing realization that the retention of a hereditary and privileged warrior class was not compatible with the formation of a modern industrialized society. Various edicts issued by the Emperor between 1873 and '76 abolished the special rights of the* samaurai *and they ceased to exist in their original form, although some of their traditions, concepts and military skills were retained. How well later generations absorbed the martial arts of the* samaurai *culture is proved by Alvin Dustine "Cap" Fog having received instruction similar to that given to his paternal grandfather from a kinsman of Tommy Okasi who lived in the United States from 1910.*

27. *The members of the Hardin, Fog and Blaze clan with whom we have been in contact cannot, or* will not, *make any statement upon the exact relationship between Elizabeth "Betty" and General Hardin. She appears in:* Part Five, "A Time For Improvisation, Mr. Blaze," J.T.'s HUNDREDTH: Part Four, "It's Our Turn to Improvise, Miss Blaze," J.T.'S LADIES; KILL DUSTY FOG; THE BAD BUNCH; McGRAW's INHERITANCE; Part Two, "The Quartet," THE HALF BREED; MASTER OF TRIGGERNOMETRY; THE RIO HONDO WAR *and* GUNSMOKE THUNDER.

Appendix Two

Raven Head, only daughter of Chief Long Walker, war leader of the *Pehnane*—Wasp, Quick Stinger, Raider—Comanches' Dog Soldier lodge and his French Creole *pairaivo*,[1] married an Irish Kentuckian adventurer, Sam Ysabel, but died giving birth to their first child. Baptized "Loncey Dalton," the boy was raised after the fashion of the *Nemenuh*.[2] With his father away upon the family's combined business of mustanging—catching, breaking wild horses[3] and smuggling, his education was left largely in the hands of his maternal grandfather.[4] From Long Walker, he learned all those things a Comanche warrior must know: how to ride the wildest freshly caught mustang, or make a trained animal subservient to his will when "raiding"—a polite name for the favorite pastime of the male *Nemenuh*, stealing horses—to follow the faintest tracks and just as effectively conceal signs of his own passing; to locate hidden enemies, or to keep out of sight himself should the need arise; to know the ways of wild animals and, in some cases, imitate their calls so even others of their own kind might be fooled.[5]

The boy proved himself an excellent pupil in each subject. He had inherited his father's Kentuckian skill at rifle shooting and, while not *real* fast on the draw—taking slightly over a second to bring out and fire his weapon, whereas a top hand could practically halve that time—he performed passably with his Colt Second Model Dragoon revolver. He had won his *Pehnane* man-name, *Cuchilo*—Spanish for "Knife"—by his exceptional skill at wielding one. It was claimed by those who were best qualified to know that he would equal the alleged designer in performing with the massive, clip pointed type of blade which bore Colonel James Bowie's name.[6]

Joining his father on smuggling expeditions along the Rio Grande, the boy had become known to the Mexicans of the border country as *Cabrito;* a name which, although meaning a young goat, had arisen out of hearing white men refer to him as the Ysabel Kid and was spoken *very* respectfully in such a context. The roughest and the toughest of the bloody border's brood had soon come to acknowledge it did not pay to rile up Sam Ysabel's son. The education and upbringing of the Kid had not been calculated to develop any over-inflated sense of the sanctity of human life. When crossed, he dealt with the situation like a *Pehnane* Dog Soldier—to which war lodge of savage and most efficient warriors he had earned initiation—swiftly and in an effectively deadly manner.

During the War Between The States, the Kid and his father had first ridden as scouts for Colonel John Singleton "the Grey Ghost" Mosby. Later, their specialized knowledge and talents were diverted to having them collect and deliver to the Confederate States' authorities in Texas supplies which had been run through the blockade imposed by the United States' Navy into Matamoros, or which had been purchased in other parts in Mexico. It was hard and dangerous work, but never more so than on the two occasions they had become involved in missions with Belle "the Rebel Spy" Boyd,[7] *q.v.*

Soon after the War ended, Sam Ysabel was murdered. While hunting the killers, the Kid had met Dusty Fog and Mark Counter.[8] When the assignment upon which they were engaged came to its successful conclusion, learning the Kid no longer wished to continue smuggling or mustanging, Dusty had offered him employment at the OD Connected ranch. It had been in the capacity of scout rather than cowhand and his talents were frequently of great use as a member of the floating outfit. His acceptance had been of great benefit all round. The ranch had obtained the services of an extremely capable man. Dusty acquired a loyal friend who would stick by him through any danger.[9] For his part, the Kid was turned from a life of petty crime—with the ever present possibility of having his activities develop into serious law breaking—and became a useful member of society. Peace officers and honest citizens might have found cause to feel thankful for that.[10] His *Pehnane* education would have made him a terrible and murderous outlaw if he had been driven to a life of crime.

Obtaining his first repeating rifle—a Winchester Model of 1866, nicknamed the "Old Yellowboy" because of its brass frame, although at first it was known as the "New Improved Henry"—while in Mexico with Dusty and Mark, the Kid had soon become a master in its use. At the first Cochise County Fair, he had won first prize in the rifle shooting competition against stiff opposition.[11] It was one of the legendary Winchester Model of 1873's which qualified for the name, "One Of A Thousand."[12]

In part, it was through the efforts of the Kid that the majority of the Comanche bands had agreed to go on to the reservation, following the attempts to ruin the treaty signing ceremony at Fort Sorrel being circumvented.[13] Nor could Dusty have cleaned out the outlaw town called "Hell" without him.[14] He had also accompanied Miss Martha "Calamity Jane" Canary when she went to claim a ranch she had inherited.[15]

---

1. Pairaivo, *first, or favorite, wife. As is the case with other Comanche terms, this is a phonetic spelling.*
2. Nemenuh: *"The People," the Comanches' name for their nation. Members of other Indian races with whom they came into contact called them, frequently with good cause, Tshaoh, "the Enemy People."*
3. *A description of the work of a party of mustangers is given in:* .44 CALIBER MAN *and* A HORSE CALLED MOGOLLON.
4. *Told in:* COMANCHE.
5. *An example of how the Ysabel Kid turned his knowledge of wild animals to good use is given in:* Part Three, "A Wolf's A Knowing Critter," J.T.'S HUNDRETH.
6. *Some researchers claim the actual designer of the knife was James*

Bowie's eldest brother, Rezin Pleasant and was made by the master cutler, James Black of Arkansas. (A few authorities state it was manufactured by Jesse Cliffe, a white blacksmith employed on the Bowie family's plantation in Rapides Parish, (Louisiana). As all James Black's knives were hand made, there were variations in their dimensions. The specimen owned by the Ysabel Kid had a blade eleven and a half inches long, two and a half inches wide and a quarter of an inch thick at the guard. One thing all "bowie" knives have in common is a "clip" point, where the last few inches of the otherwise unsharpened "back" of the blade joins and becomes an extension of the main cutting surface in a concave arc, whereas a "spear" point is formed by the two sides coming together in symmetrical curves. What happened to James Bowie's knife after his death in the final assault of the siege of the Alamo Mission, at San Antonio de Bexar, Texas, on March the 6th, 1836, is told in: GET URREA and THE QUEST FOR BOWIE'S BLADE.

7. Told in: THE BLOODY BORDER and BACK TO THE BLOODY BORDER. (Berkley Books, U.S.A., 1978 re-titled, RENEGADE.)

8. Told in: THE YSABEL KID.

9. A similar association was formed between a grandson of the Ysabel Kid, Mark Scrapton, and Alvin Dustine "Cap" Fog, q.v., as is told in: RAPIDO CLINT, MORE JUSTICE FROM COMPANY "Z" and THE JUSTICE OF COMPANY "Z."

10. One young woman certainly had cause for gratitude as is told in: Part Three, "Sam Ysabel's Son,' THE TEXAN and its "expansion," OLD MOCCASINS ON THE TRAIL.

11. Told in: GUN WIZARD.

12. When manufacturing the extremely popular Winchester Model of 1873 rifle, the makers selected those having barrels found to shoot with exceptional accuracy to be fitted with set triggers and given a special fine finish. Originally, these were inscribed, "1 of 1,000," but this was later changed to script, "One Of A Thousand." The title was, however, a considerable understatement as only one hundred and thirty-six out of a total production of 720,610 rifles qualified for the distinction. Those of a grade lower in quality were given the name "One Of A Hundred," but only seven were so designated. The practice commenced in 1875 and was discontinued in 1878, allegedly because the management decided it was not good policy to suggest the Company produced different grades of gun.

13. Told in: SIDEWINDER.

14. Told in: HELL IN THE PALO DURO and GO BACK TO HELL.

15. Told in: WHITE STALLION, RED MARE.

Appendix Three

During the years we have been writing, we have frequently received letters asking for various Western terms, or incidents to which we refer, to be explained in greater detail. While we do not have the slightest objection to receiving such mail, we have found it saves much time consuming repetition to include those most often requested in each volume. Our "old hands" have seen them before, but there are always "new chums" coming along who have not.

1. Although Americans in general used the word, "cinch," from the Spanish, "cincha," for the short band made from coarsely woven horsehair, canvas, or cordage, and terminated at each end with a metal ring which—together with the latigo—is used to fasten the saddle on the back of a horse, because of its Mexican connotations, Texans employ the term, "girth," generally pronouncing it "girt." As cowhands of the Lone Star State fastened the end of the lariat to the saddlehorn when roping the half wild longhorn cattle, or range horses, instead of using a "dally" which could be slipped free hurriedly in an emergency, their rigs had two girths for added security.

2. "Light a shuck:" cowhands' expression for leaving hurriedly. It derives from the habit in the night camps of trail drives or roundups on the open range of supplying "shucks"—dried corn cobs—to be lit and used as illumination by anybody who had to leave the camp-fire and walk in the darkness. As the "shuck" burned away very quickly, a person had to move fast if wanting to benefit from its light.

3. "Make wolf bait:" one term meaning to kill. It derived from the practice in the Old West, when a range was infested by predators—not necessarily just wolves—of slaughtering an animal and, poisoning the carcass, leaving it to be devoured.

4. We strongly suspect the trend in film and television Westerns made

since the early 1960's to portray all cowhands as long haired, heavily bearded and filthy stems less from the desire of the production companies to create "realism" than because there were so few actors— particularly to play supporting roles—who were short haired and clean shaven and because the "liberal" elements who began to gain control of the entertainment media appear to have an obsession for showing dirty habits, conditions and appearances. In our extensive reference library, we cannot find a dozen photographs of actual cowhands—as opposed to Army Scouts, mountain men, or old time gold prospectors—with long hair and bushy beards. In fact, our reading on the subject has led us to assume the term "long hair" was one of opprobrium in the cattle country of the Old West and Prohibition eras as it still is today.

5. The sharp toes and high heels of the boots worn by cowhands were purely functional. The former could enter, or be slipped free from a stirrup iron very quickly in an emergency. Not only did the latter offer a firmer grip in the stirrups, they could be spiked into the ground to supply extra holding power when roping on foot.

6. "Gone to Texas:" at odds with the law, usually in the United States of America at the time the saying came into being. Many fugitives from justice entered Texas during the colonization period—which commenced in the early 1820's due to the Government of Mexico offering land to "Anglos" so they could act as a "buffer state" against the marauding Comanche Indians—and continued until annexation as a State of the Union on February the 16th, 1846. Until the latter became a fact, such miscreants had known there was little danger of being arrested and extradited by the local authorities. In fact, like Kenya from the 1920's until the outbreak of World War II, in spite of the great number of honest, law-abiding and hard working folks who genuinely wished to make their home there, Texas in the days before independence was attained from Mexican domination, gained a reputation for being a "place in the sun for shady people."

7. Give it up to the Green River:" another term meaning to kill, generally with some form of edged weapon. First produced on the Green River, at Green Field, Massachusetts in 1834, a very popular knife had the following inscription on the blade just below the hilt, "J. Russell & Co./Green River Works." Any weapon thrust into an enemy "up to the Green River" would almost certainly inflict a fatal wound whether it bore the inscription or not.

8. "Mason-Dixon" line, also erroneously called the "Mason-Dixie line:" the boundary between Pennsylvania and Maryland, as surveyed in 1763–67 by the Englishmen, Charles Mason and Jeremiah Dixon, which came to be regarded as the dividing line separating the Southern "Slave" from the Northern "Free" States.

9. *"New England:" the North-East section of the United States of America, including Massachusetts, New Hampshire, Maine, Vermont, Connecticut and Rhode Island, which was first settled primarily by people from the British Isles.*

10. *In the Old West, the jurisdiction of various types of law enforcement agencies was restricted as follows: town marshal, confined to the town or city which hired him; sheriff, to his own county; Texas or Arizona Rangers could go anywhere in their respective State, although the former were technically required to await invitation by the local authorities before participating in an investigation; United States marshal could go anywhere in the country, but was only intended to become involved in "Federal" crimes.*

For Brigadier J.R. Spurry, C.B.E., M.R.C.V.S.,
R.A.V.C., without whose kind acceptance of my
story once in Kenya, justice would have been done—
and so would I!

This Berkley book contains the complete
text of the original edition.
It has been completely reset in a typeface
designed for easy reading, and was printed
from new film.

WHITE INDIANS

A Berkley Book/published by arrangement with
Transworld Publishers Ltd.

PRINTING HISTORY
Corgi edition published 1982
Berkley edition/September 1985

ISBN: 0-425-08086-2

A BERKLEY BOOK® TM 757,375
Berkley Books are published by The Berkley Publishing Group,
200 Madison Avenue, New York, New York 10016.
The name "BERKLEY" and the stylized "B"
with design are trademarks belonging to
Berkley Publishing Corporation.
PRINTED IN THE UNITED STATES OF AMERICA

J.T. Edson

WHITE INDIANS

BERKLEY BOOKS, NEW YORK